Give the Lady a Ride

holding a glass of lemonade, and rocking on the porch while the sun kissed the earth goodnight.

Once inside the front door, though, she cringed. Wallpaper with massive globs of olive green leaves and dusty pink flowers buckled and peeled from the walls. The white linoleum floor had faded to a dull yellow everywhere it wasn't scuffed bare. Room after room of drab, functional furniture. Plaid draperies parted over grimy windows. Western art of questionable quality adorned the walls. The entire house begged for an interior decorator.

"It's not *too* bad." Marie Lambeau, her best friend and roommate, eyed the kitchen's gold appliances and stained countertops.

"It's a bit rough," Patricia whispered. The cowboy stood at the door behind them like a sentry guarding the palace jewels.

"Well, it's not like you're going to use it. You can't even boil water." Marie glanced over her shoulder. "Though if you hook up with that dark, handsome novelty over there, you'll have to learn."

Patricia leveled a gaze at her friend. "Don't get ideas about matching me with him. I'm putting this place on the market first thing Monday morning, and he's not likely to find that endearing."

Marie held up hands of innocence. "I wouldn't try to fix you up with anyone."

"Sure you would." Patricia laughed. "You can't help it. It's what you do."

At the far end of the narrow kitchen, a door led to a stocked pantry, and another to the laundry room. Back home, Melba had always done the cooking and laundry when Patricia was growing up, and although she'd watched occasionally, domestic chores

4

remained a mystery she didn't care to solve. If any cooking was done in the apartment they shared in New York, Marie had the honors. A maid cleaned the place once a week, and as for the dirty laundry–that was why cleaners were invented.

She turned to the cowboy. "I've seen enough of the house now. Could you show me the books, Mr. . . . I'm sorry, I don't know your name."

Before he could speak, a screen door slammed and a masculine voice shouted, "Talon! You in here?"

"Kitchen!" he yelled over his shoulder, then delivered a tight-lipped nod to Patricia. "Talon Carlson, ma'am, foreman of the Circle Bar. And I'd like to see your papers before I show you the finances."

She tilted her head, taking in the thrum of the pulse in his left temple, the angry crease in his brow bisecting the tan line made by his hat. Just who did he think he was? Did he *know* who she was? She could give him a swift lesson, but then, how impressive would a New York senator's daughter be in Texas? Judging from the steel in those dark brown eyes, the President of the United States wouldn't impress him.

The other man entered the room and jerked the cap off his sandy blond head the moment he saw her.

"Excuse me, ma'am, sorry for the interruption." He locked eyes with Marie, and his neck reddened to his ears.

"What do you need, Chance?" Talon growled.

"Uh . . ." Chance dragged his gaze away from Marie. "Yeah, uh, Bodine's out again."

"Good grief." Talon about-faced and strode out of the kitchen. Chance flashed them a smile then followed, jamming his cap back on his head.

"Who's Bodine?" Patricia asked Marie.

Marie craned her neck to watch the men exit the house. "Who's Chance?"

Talon quick-stepped across the gravel drive to the gate in front of the horse barn. Behind the barn, his ancient quarter horse hobbled around the paddock. The buckskin was supposed to remain confined to his stall until the wound on his left foreleg healed. "How'd he get out this time?"

"Same way he always does. He just opened his stall and left before any of us noticed." Chance followed Talon through the gate and matched stride with him as they headed for the barn. "Who are those women?"

Talon grabbed a halter from the tack room and a handful of sugar cubes from the coffee stand, then marched out the back. His head still reeled from Jake's betrayal. He had given the ranch to a total stranger. A woman. A Yankee woman, with polished nails and soft hands.

"You gonna tell me?"

"The blonde's Patricia Talbert. I didn't catch the other's name."

"Okay. But who are they?"

"Ms. Talbert says she's the new owner." The words almost choked him.

Chance halted. "Did I hear you right?"

Talon nodded, not daring to speak. They were closer to the horse now. If Bodine heard anger in Talon's voice, he'd shy away. Maybe hurt himself worse.

Talon sucked in a breath of spring hay and horsehide and

forced his temper down. He had no reason to be angry. He knew this was coming, had known since Jake died a month ago that things were going to change.

He softened his voice for the sake of his horse. "Easy, boy. Out for an afternoon stroll?"

Bodine nickered and shook his dark mane. He limped toward them, stretching his neck to sniff the sugar in Talon's palm. Talon eased closer and opened his fingers so his old mount could lip up the snack, then slipped the halter over the horse's ears and rubbed his neck.

Chance held the lead rope as Talon slid his hand down the bandaged foreleg. Bodine's withers flinched. How he had managed to come out this far was a mystery, but it couldn't happen again. Not if that leg was to heal. Talon straightened and led the horse on a slow trek to the barn.

Chance joined him, with Bodine between them bobbing his head to the beat of their footsteps. "So, Ms. Talbert inherited the place?"

"I guess. I'd like some proof though before I turn her loose with the finances." But he shouldn't have been so rude to her when she'd asked. Lord, please forgive him. He knew better than to act like that.

"How did she know the McAllisters?"

"I don't know, we didn't get that far. Maybe she's the kinfolk Jake's lawyer mentioned. I just wish he'd mentioned she was female. I wouldn't have been so surprised." He stopped near the barn's back entry and tied Bodine's rope on a rail near a grassy patch. "Guess I was more surprised to learn Jake and Loretta had any living kinfolk."

"Yeah, me too. I always assumed you'd get the ranch."

Talon's lips pursed. He'd also presumed he'd inherit the ranch. Or maybe he'd just dreamed it so hard, he'd lost all sense of reality. Jake had always treated him like a son; Talon had always loved and respected the man as a father. When Jake made him foreman, the dreams began to root.

But the pain of a shattered dream had eased a bit. That Jake would want to give the ranch to a blood relative made sense. Even to a woman who wouldn't know how to run it. Talon snorted. "We can always hope she'll be an absentee owner."

"That'd work." Chance grinned over Bodine's back. "Reckon she'll keep you as boss?"

Talon stared at the grass. Losing his job wasn't something he'd considered. If he kept spurring the bad side of the new owner, that just might be his fate. He really needed to work on his temper.

As Patricia turned the Mercedes onto the county road, Marie peered out the windshield at the acres of red and brown cattle with their noses deep in the fresh grass and purple vetch. "Where are you going to find a fax machine in this barren country?"

"In town. It isn't as backward as you think. They have a great little café that makes the best pies in the world. Meringue this high." Patricia spread her thumb and forefinger four inches apart. She turned left at a blinking light and headed down the blacktop. "But the town has changed a lot since I was here as a kid. It's livelier."

Marie lowered her Gucci shades and gawked at her over the rims. "You call this lively? Wake up, woman! You're from New York!"

Give the Lady a Ride

"Yeah, I am." Patricia leaned her left elbow against the car door. "Do you know what dawned on me at the Circle Bar? I'm anonymous in Texas. Even the senator has little influence here."

Marie shot her a skeptical look. "And this is a good thing?"

"Well, it would be nice to have actual friends and not just a bunch of political junkies wanting to meet my father." She rolled her eyes over to Marie. "Present company excepted, that is."

"Oh, c'mon. What makes you think you don't have actual friends?"

"I have evidence."

Marie's eyes narrowed. "Ever since Kent told you he'd married you to get to your father, you've questioned every friendship. He really rattled you."

"Don't go there." Patricia bristled at the mention of her late husband—a man who would've been her *ex*-husband if not for a fatal accident five years ago. "I don't want to talk about him."

"But he's the reason you've lost faith in yourself, in your ability to judge character." Marie twisted in the seat to face her. "Every time you meet new people, his words spring out of nowhere like they just popped from his mouth yesterday. And they still have the power to slap you down."

"I said I didn't want to talk about it."

"Fine." Marie settled back, but kept her eyes on Patricia. "The point is, you *have* actual friends. Not everyone you hang out with is involved in politics. Most of them don't care who your father is."

"Oh, please! Just last week, Lisa wanted to know if Dad could fix a ticket. Martin wanted me to present an idea for energy conservation. And Vince!" Her left hand shot toward the roof.

"He's aiming to be a state senator and wants Dad's endorsement."

Marie's lips parted in surprise. "When did he decide he wanted to be a senator?"

"Get this. He's been thinking about it for *years*. Which makes me wonder if that's not why Tracie introduced him to me. She wasn't fixing me up on a blind date. She was fixing him up for a trip to Albany." She glared out the window. "Sometimes I want to get away from all of them. I want to hide somewhere. Just say goodbye to New York and start over somewhere else."

"Where would you go? Here? Do you want to move here?"

"Sure, why not? Cattle are far less complicated creatures to deal with. Maybe it wouldn't be such a bad idea." She turned the car down the town's short main drag with its dusty streets and Wild West storefronts.

"Maybe you *should* move to Texas." Marie spread her arms wide at the rustic scene beyond the windshield. "Who would want to leave all this?"

Patricia tossed her a dry smile and maneuvered the car past a construction site where one of the stores was getting a facelift, then parked in front of the Chamber of Commerce. "If they don't have a fax machine here, maybe they can tell us where we can find one."

They parked the car and approached the chamber's double doors. Colorful posters on the glass advertised an upcoming Texas Steak Cook-Off. Judging by the snapshots from last year, the annual event was a major one for the small town.

"That might be fun." Marie bent for a closer look at one of the pictures.

"We won't be here."

Give the Lady a Ride

"I thought you said you might want to stay."

"I wasn't serious." Patricia's gaze wandered to a rodeo poster on the bottom left panel. The three-day event would start tonight and continue through the weekend. She rapped a knuckle against the glass. "I know we'll be here for this. Let's go tonight. It'll be fun."

Marie wrinkled her nose. "You must be kidding."

Talon leaned against a cedar post on the bunkhouse porch with his boots crossed and his thumbs hooked in his front pockets. The faces of the five cowhands in the yard drooped worse than bloodhounds' muzzles, and he could tell they hadn't liked what they'd heard so far about the new owner. The two younger men, Jack Billings and Randy Sweeney, studied the ground near Talon's feet. Frank Simmons stared into the distance and stroked his shaggy, iron-gray mustache. Buster Milligan's lighter gray brows knit together like two caterpillars dancing the hula.

"I don't know anything else right now. She was gone by the time I got back from the barn. But let me tell you this . . ." Talon pushed away from the post, set his legs wide, and folded his arms. "You work for this ranch, this brand, regardless of who the owner is. I don't know where she's from, but she ain't from here. She won't know beans about ranching. And she'd have a hard time replacing this crew. So unless you simply can't stomach working for a woman, do your job. Just swallow hard and get 'er done."

"Reckon that's all we can do." Buster slid his hat off and wiped his balding head with a blue paisley kerchief. "Not like we have any place to go."

"Won't be so bad having a pretty boss for a change." Frank's eyes shifted back to Talon from whatever he'd stared at before. "Besides, she may be a plus in our favor. As long as she owns the ranch, she'll need us. If the Circle Bar'd gone to another rancher with his own crew, might be we'd all lose our jobs. 'Course, if she sells, we might still be out of our jobs."

Talon hadn't thought of that, and the realization kicked him like a rodeo bronc. He couldn't imagine working anywhere else, didn't *want* to work anywhere else. The Circle Bar was all he'd ever wanted, and the idea she'd sell it out from under them churned in his stomach hotter than jalapeños.

Chance shrugged. "But, like you said, as long as she owns it, she'll need us. What'll she know about running a ranch?"

"Nothing. I know absolutely nothing about ranching." Patricia turned onto the highway and drove back to the Circle Bar. The facsimile of the property deed was folded neatly in her purse, ready for round two with the cowboy. "What was Uncle Jake thinking? I can't run a ranch."

"How hard can it be?" Marie waved a dismissive hand. "It's the same as running any other business."

"But I don't run a business. I'm Dad's social coordinator. There isn't much in common between the two."

"Okay, look at it this way. You have a bunch o' hunks out there that *do* know how to run a ranch. Just kick back and let them do it."

"But I'd have to live in Texas. I'd hate living in Texas."

"Uh-huh. Not one hour ago you were singing the praises of

anonymity."

"Yeah, and not one hour ago, you were making fun of how small the town is. And you're right. Few restaurants, no clubs, no concert halls–not even a movie theater!"

"And yet you've found nothing to complain about other than the ranch house. You have become so indecisive, I barely recognize you."

Marie had a point. Indecisiveness was another effect of Patricia's failed marriage. The one she didn't want to think about. "Okay, how's this? I am going to sell the ranch. Dad needs me for his campaign. I must get back."

At the sound of gravel pinging against a back fender, Talon rose from the porch rocker at the main house and looked toward the car speeding down the white caliche road.

So they were back. Proof of ownership in hand, no doubt. He hadn't realized he'd been hanging on to the hope that it was all a big mistake. He remembered his words to the men earlier: Swallow hard. Time for a change in his attitude. He needed to keep his *aw-shucks* grin handy and his thoughts to himself.

According to the Timex on his wrist, it was four o'clock. She'd barely left him any time this afternoon to move his mind in the direction of his bull ride in tonight's competition. He wanted his shot at the silver buckle and the thousand dollar purse.

At one time, the prize would've been added to the seed money Talon had been saving to bring his plans for this ranch into reality. Things like getting a computer. He'd seen ranch-management software that would simplify the record keeping, and he wanted it. But Jake had resisted computers and twenty-first century technology in general. If it hadn't come equipped with a steering wheel, Jake hadn't wanted it. His only exceptions had been the phone and TV. Whipping the Circle Bar into the new century had been Talon's goal–until he realized he would never own the ranch.

The Yankee woman in that gravel-kicking Mercedes owned it.

The car crunched to a stop in the drive, and the women emerged from it with refined grace. The sun caught Ms. Talbert's hair, causing it to shine and Talon's mood to lighten. Ms. Talbert was a cute little thing, trim and petite in her blue slacks and flowered pullover. Her blonde hair blew in the breeze as soft as the willows by the creek. Frank was right. Maybe it would be good to have a pretty boss for a change. As long as she let him be the foreman.

He slid his grin into place. "Welcome back."

"Thank you." Her smile was stiff and reserved, all business. She took her work seriously. He could respect that.

Her friend, a good four inches taller, glanced back at the men in the corral before she marched up the steps and shoved out her hand. "I didn't introduce myself earlier. I'm Marie Lambeau. I don't have a thing to do with this business, I'm just happy to be here."

He had to smile at her enthusiasm, although she was undoubtedly more interested in meeting Chance than anything else. He'd seen the way she looked at him earlier. Maybe she wanted Talon to hook them up. A little adolescent, but charming just the same.

"I have the deed right here." Ms. Talbert pulled the papers

Give the Lady a Ride

from her purse. "If it passes your inspection, perhaps you can show me the books now."

He took the slick folded sheets and opened them. Sure enough. In big, bold, smeared letters. The lady owned the ranch. "Well, good for you, ma'am. The Circle Bar's a great spread."

"Thank you. And please don't call me ma'am." She climbed the steps and took the deed from him. "Now, the books?"

He held the screen door open, then followed them into the house.

"I'll be glad to show you the financial side of the business today, but tomorrow would be better. I'll have a little more time." At Ms. Talbert's questioning gaze, he added, "I have to ride tonight, ma'am. I need to be getting myself ready."

"Ride?" Marie's warm brown eyes lit up.

"Yes, ma'am. I'm in the rodeo this weekend."

She stole another peek at the men outside. "Is, um, is anyone else from the ranch riding?"

He swallowed his chuckle at her barely hidden message. "Just Chance and me, ma'am."

Give the Lady a Ride

Chapter Two

The barrel racing event, in full swing on the arena floor, served as warning for the bull riders to prepare. In the locker room, cowboys strapped on chaps, rosined ropes, buckled on spurs, and slipped into protective vests. Talon cinched his spur strap, then pulled his rosin and rope from his gear bag. Chance dropped onto the wooden bench beside him.

"Which bull did you draw?" Talon stood to loop the rope over a nail in the wall.

"Hopeless Ride." Chance sounded as excited as a kid in the doctor's office. "I just hope he puts on a good show."

Hopeless was an unpredictable bull, a bad draw. He could be rough on the cowboy, or too easy to score well. One time, he had dropped to his knees in the chute, and all the spurring in the world hadn't forced him up. Chance needed Hopeless to bring his A-game.

"Maybe he'll give you a good run." Talon opened the rosin and set to work rubbing the sticky substance into his braided nylon rope. "You'll have to put on a show. The new boss is here with that friend of hers, Marie Lambeau." He waggled his brows. "She seems to have a thing for you."

"You think she likes me?" Chance's neck flushed. Being a fair-haired cowboy didn't do him any favors. He burned crimson in the summer and blushed like a happy toddler the rest of time. Keeping his thoughts to himself was just short of impossible.

"The woman's smitten. Just crook your finger and she'll come a'runnin'!" Talon tossed the rosin to Chance and coiled his rope, grinning at the redness drifting up Chance's cheeks.

The first rider's name blared over the speakers. The event was starting, and Talon's turn would soon be up. He draped the looped coils over his shoulder, shoved his hat tighter on his head, and grabbed his riding glove and mouth guard. "Bet you're glad those women are here now, aren't ya?"

Chance snapped a towel at him, nicking his thigh as he headed out. "Good luck."

Talon flicked a two-fingered wave over his shoulder and waded through contestants and officials on his way to the chutes. He shook his head, grinning over his friend's reaction to a little teasing about Marie. Unlike Talon, Chance had always been able to meet a prospective relationship with open arms. He preferred the company of Christian ladies, but those who weren't saved when they'd met, he had introduced to the Lord by the time they parted. The way Marie had eyed Talon from the front porch, she wasn't likely a Christian. Chance would have his work cut out for him.

Every relationship Talon had entered had ended badly, until he finally got the point: for whatever reason, God wanted him single, and Talon intended to be obedient. Eight years ago, he'd stuffed away his dreams of having a family of his own. Even if he were like Chance and able to enjoy a new attraction, he would still have no possibility of a relationship–especially not with a lady as attractive as Patricia Talbert.

The idea was moot anyway. She was his boss.

The sight of the chutes jerked him back to the present. He needed to focus. He had drawn Ransom, a broad, bulky bull that could twist like a rattler.

Buster waited for him on the wooden platform behind chute four. Talon gave him the rope to wrap around the bull, then wrangled his hand into his leather glove.

Buster slapped his back. "You ready?"

"Ready as I'll ever be." He lowered his gaze away from Buster's upraised brows. Talon's usual response to the question was, *ya betcha!* But that was when he wasn't distracted by thoughts of beautiful ladies and pointless relationships. The best he could say for himself now was that his spurs were on straight.

Squirming on the hard aluminum bench, Patricia ground dirt into her Ralph Lauren slacks as she tried to see around the broad-brimmed hat on the man in front of her. If she leaned just so—and if the man wouldn't move—she could see Talon in the chute.

Marie slid a soda straw from her lips and rattled the ice in the sweaty paper cup. "Admit it. You think he's cute. If we weren't leaving Tuesday, you'd go after him."

"No, I wouldn't. I'm not interested. I just want to watch him ride."

"Uh-huh."

Patricia saw no point in arguing, especially if she couldn't sound convincing. She did find Talon attractive. Before the rodeo, she'd seen him walking toward the arena with a green nylon bag slung over one broad shoulder, and his hat square on his head. He wasn't a giant of a man, but his long stride emanated confidence. In the shade of the pavilion, he hadn't seemed as arrogant as he had at the ranch. Purposeful, perhaps; directed. His dark eyes were serious and focused on some inner thought, but when another cowboy greeted him, his smile was immediate and genuine.

A genuine smile was unheard of in her political world. For that alone, she'd be interested–if she were to ever play the dating game again. Which she wouldn't.

When the first ride ended and the score was called, the arena announcer broadcast Talon's name over the P.A. system. "Talon's riding *Ransom*. This high kicker'd just as soon stomp on ya as to look at ya. The cowboy's got his hands full tonight!"

On the sandy floor below, a long-legged cowboy yanked open the chute gate, and a monster of a bull lunged into the arena with a leap a gymnast would envy. His hindquarters twisted in a roll, exposing his chalky white belly. Talon kept his left hand up as the bull landed on its front hooves. The animal curled to the right like a banner in the wind before its back hooves hit the dirt. Talon listed, jerking into balance an instant before the bull thrust to the left. His arm slashed the air, his body wrenched with spine-snapping jolts each time the bull thrashed.

Patricia tucked her bottom lip between her teeth. The man had seemed so invincible earlier; now he looked like a threadbare rag doll. Each time his body lurched, she flinched. He must've been insane to strap himself onto such a beast.

The eight-second horn blasted, and the announcer's words, *qualified round,* echoed in the arena. Patricia's breath shot through her lips. The ride was over. Talon was safe.

Then the bull's final kick sent him flying, and he crashed

several yards away.

Ransom turned, lowered his hornless head, and charged.

With her heart in her throat and her fist at her lips, Patricia willed Talon to get up. He was too slow rising from the dust. He should've scrambled to the rails as the other riders had before him. He should've run. He should've at least been on his feet. Instead, he sat with a hand to his head an instant away from the bull's thundering hooves.

A blur of men in bright red and blue shirts rushed the animal, stealing its attention. Ransom turned mid-stride and rammed one of the red-shirted bullfighters in the stomach, tossing him aside like an old newspaper. The bullfighter popped back up and resumed the chase. Patricia's eyes widened. A hit that hard should've sent the man to the emergency room.

On the far side of the arena, Talon staggered to the rails and clung to them, watching over his shoulder as the bullfighters drove the animal to the pen behind the chutes. Once the sand was clear, Talon dropped down to one knee and bowed his head, then rose and pointed to the sky. Someone offered him his hat, and after a quick wave to the crowd, he disappeared into the web of rails and pens.

He'd walked out on his own two feet. *This* time. No wonder he'd prayed, probably thanking God he hadn't been pulverized by hooves.

Without a doubt, the man was insane.

Chapter Three

The sun glared through the crack in the faded burgundy motel curtains and beamed straight into Patricia's eyes. She groaned and rolled over on the lumpy king-sized mattress to shake Marie awake. "We need to start moving. I have to go through the ranch records today."

Marie grumbled into her pillow and burrowed further under the covers.

"Fine." Patricia rolled off the bed and went to the bathroom. At least with Marie asleep, she wouldn't have to rush her shower.

Twenty minutes later, after getting pelted and revitalized by the hard water, she wrapped herself in a towel. Marie had sprawled diagonally across the mattress and was softly snoring. Without making a sound, Patricia slipped on some clothes, then threw her wet towel over Marie's face.

"Hey!" Marie shot upright and whisked the towel away.

Patricia laughed. "You'd better get up or I'm going to leave you here all day."

"Fine with me." She balled up the towel and threw it back.

"I'll sleep."

"Uh-huh. For another thirty minutes. You'll be wide awake before long and stuck here for hours. Just you and daytime TV." Marie pulled a pillow over her head, so Patricia raised her voice. "No–worse. *Saturday* TV. Golf. Baseball. NASCAR."

"I'm up. I'm up." Marie flung the pillow aside. "Get me coffee."

"You'll have to dress first. The best coffee is at the café."

Marie yawned and arched her back like a stretching cat. "I feel like I've been beaten with a sledge hammer."

"It's not the most comfortable mattress. Want to stay in Stephenville tonight?"

"Would it be any better?"

"Won't know if we don't try." Patricia grabbed her blow dryer. "Did you see Talon praying last night?"

"After his ride? Sure. Chance prayed too. Probably thankful they didn't get killed." Marie swung her legs over the side of the bed and rose. "If you ask me, it was out of place. Religion is private. It shouldn't be a spectator sport."

She disappeared into the bathroom. Patricia bent forward, flipping her hair over her head, and switched on the dryer.

Perhaps Marie was right. People shouldn't display their Christianity. The Supreme Court seemed to agree. But when Patricia had been saved as a kid, she'd found it almost impossible to contain her newfound faith. She was certainly able to keep it under wraps now. In her position, she couldn't run the risk of offending anyone. Her own faith was so deeply hidden, she wasn't sure it was still there. That Talon had prayed openly last night, unconcerned with what others would think, was . . . *alien* to her.

Give the Lady a Ride

"Are we going back to the arena tonight?" Marie called through the door.

"I thought the rodeo was beneath you."

"Don't hold my ignorance against me. I didn't know how much fun it would be." Marie poked her head out and grinned. "Besides, Chance beat Talon last night. I want to watch him do it again."

"You just want to watch *him*."

"Yeah. What's your point?" Marie closed herself inside the bathroom again. "Nothing like a denim-clad distraction to make this trip seem worthwhile."

"You're incorrigible!" But maybe that was why Patricia was so eager to get to the ranch. Anxious to see her own denim-clad distraction.

She scowled at her reflection. She was here to sell the ranch, not fall for its foreman.

Talon jumped into the cab of his Dodge Ram and slammed the door with a fury fitting his mood. It was ten o'clock. Ten o'-blasted-clock! The auction would start at eleven, and the culled cattle should've been there hours ago.

The truck bounced and swayed with each calf that was crowded into the trailer behind him. Chance had already pulled out with a trailer-load of calves, but his few minutes head start wouldn't save him from the inevitable line at the off-loading ramp. Talon watched through his side rearview. There wasn't a man there who didn't seem like he was wading through thigh-high mud. Even the calves were slow.

Finally, Randy banged shut the trailer gate and circled a finger in the air. "Ho!"

Talon fired up the engine and lurched away from the loading chute. He eased onto the gravel driveway and got a head-on view of a silver Mercedes outrunning a dust cloud.

Spitting out a word he thought he'd long ago yanked from his vocabulary, Talon pulled over to the grass. He'd have to repent of his foul mood, but he might as well wait and see just how foul it was going to get.

The car stopped abreast of the truck, and Ms. Talbert's window lowered.

"Where are you going? You're supposed to show me the books today."

Talon glared out his windshield, clenching his jaw to keep his angry words tucked safely behind the bars of his teeth. He'd forgotten about her. In the rush of the morning, with the power outage and the flat on the trailer and the cantankerous motor in Chance's truck, he'd just plain forgotten about her.

But that wasn't her fault.

Please, Father, give me patience. He propped his forearm along the open truck window and leaned out. "Ma'am, it's been a rough morning already, and I'm running late."

"Late for what?"

"Auction, ma'am. We've got to sell our culls."

"Auction?" Marie stretched over from the passenger seat and peered out at him through dark shades. "That should be fun."

Talon's right hand clenched the wheel.

"Sure," Ms. Talbert said. "Why don't we follow you there?"

He shot his breath through his teeth. "Yes, ma'am."

She was the boss. She owned the place. He worked for her.

Smile. Be nice.

Give the Lady a Ride

Lord, would he ever get used to the change?

Her Mercedes, dwarfed by the four-door pickups with their attached trailers, bounced over the ruts in the lot. Patricia finally brought it to a rest in the grass near a shoddy tan building with tinted windows. Clusters of cowboys congregated outside the double doors, and on the other side of the smoky glass, many more sat at lunch booths in the auction barn's restaurant.

Marie slid a hand over her slacks. "We seem a bit overdressed."

"You think?" Patricia's own outfit was dry-clean only. She hadn't expected to spend the day at a livestock auction.

"Oh, well, who cares?" Marie popped off her seatbelt. "We're not going to sit here all day, are we?"

By the time Patricia had joined Marie at the back of the car, Marie's eyes had zeroed in on Chance and Talon across the white-rock parking lot.

"Just remember," Patricia warned, "we're leaving Tuesday."

"I remember." As the men strode toward them, Marie sighed. "Look at them. Don't you want to gobble them up?"

"No. I just met them. And you don't have time. Weren't you listening? We are leaving in three days. Three." She held her fingers up. "No gobbling. Don't gobble!"

"Don't gobble what?" Talon stopped beside her, gracing her with one of his genuine smiles–not that silly, halfway grin he usually wore, but the real smile he'd given his friends the night before. Her heart flipped like a pancake. "You two hungry?"

"Hungry? No." She latched onto his arm and steered him toward the auction barn's entrance before Marie could pop off with whatever remark entered her head. "But I could go for some water."

Holding open one of the double doors, Talon ushered them into the chilled air. The scent of grilled steaks and hot potatoes overrode the smell of sweat, dirt, and leather. Men glanced up from under their hat brims, and Talon and Chance nodded at a few. Chance appeared so puffed-up proud to be walking with Marie, his chest seemed to arrive at the order counter a full thirty seconds before the rest of him. He tilted his head toward Talon. "I figure we'll be the talk of three counties after today."

"Why? Don't women come in here?" Patricia whispered just under the murmur of masculine voices and the clinks of forks on stoneware.

"Sure they do." Talon ordered four bottled waters from a stern-faced cook in a greasy apron. "It's just that they're usually ranchers' wives in blue jeans, not well-dressed beauties from above the Mason-Dixon Line."

"It is our duty and honor as Ambassadors from the North to spread a little culture into your dreary denim world." Putting on airs, Marie raised her chin, then she grinned. "As long as you continue to supply us with sirloins."

Chance laughed. "That'll be our pleasure."

They took their water to a nearby table. Talon held a chair out for Patricia, then flipped another around and straddled it. As he cracked open his bottle, he looked at her. "Have you ever been to an auction before, ma'am?"

"Not one quite like this." Fund-raising auctions bringing in hundreds of thousands of dollars, yes, but never in surroundings so . . . rustic. "This is a new experience for me."

"Well, we'll just have to take you on the nickel tour."

Give the Lady a Ride

"I'd enjoy that, on one condition." She glanced at him from the corner of her eye. "Call me Patricia. Not Ms. Talbert, not *ma'am*, just Patricia."

He laughed, a musical, baritone chuckle she hadn't heard from him before. "Okay, Patricia it is. Besides, I don't reckon you'd like *boss lady* any better."

She tried to smile, then studied her bottle label. Now was as good a time as any to tell him she had no intention of being his boss. "Actually, I'm going to–"

"When does the auction start?" Marie asked.

"Already has." Chance capped his bottle and stood. "You want to watch?"

She was up like a shot, but since Talon hadn't risen from his chair, Patricia remained seated.

"I have to stay close so I can move my truck to the off-load ramp," Talon said, "but you could go with them if you want."

"No, that's okay. I'll wait." Patricia turned to Marie. "Go ahead. I'll catch up with you later."

"I guess it's just you and me." Marie tucked her hand in the crook of Chance's waiting arm. She'd slipped into the role of Southern belle with all the ease of Scarlett O'Hara at a Confederate ball, and Patricia was almost jealous. But after Kent, she was far more cautious about entering relationships. No–after Kent, she hadn't *wanted* another relationship.

Without Marie's tacit support, Patricia was less comfortable disclosing her plans for the ranch. Instead, she picked at the water label. What was wrong with her? She'd held conversations with members of Congress, heads of state, foreign dignitaries– why couldn't she think of a single thing to say to a Texas cowboy? A question, maybe. Get him talking so she wouldn't have to.

Linda W. Yezak

"How many—"

"I'm sorry about—" Talon smiled. "You first."

"No, that's okay. You go ahead."

"I just wanted to apologize for snapping at you earlier. We had a rough morning, but that's no excuse."

"You snapped at me? When?"

His brow lifted slightly as if her words surprised him. "Back at the ranch, when I told you we needed to get to the auction."

"Oh, that." Patricia waved her hand. "That was tame compared to what I'm used to. In New York, people would consider you overly polite."

"So, you're from New York. How are you related to the McAllisters?"

"Uncle Jake and my father were brothers. They were raised on a small spread not far from here."

"Jake had a brother? I wonder why he never mentioned him."

"There was a rift between them, but Dad never speaks of it." She'd succeeded in pulling the label completely off the bottle and now rolled it into a straw between her fingers. "I'm still surprised I inherited the ranch. I've only been here once, when I was ten. We didn't even go to the funeral."

"That's a shame. He was a good man."

Since she'd only met her uncle that one time, she didn't know how to respond. She unrolled the label and started again from the opposite corner.

The windows rattled with the sound of diesel engines, and Talon rose. "Guess it's time to move my truck. If you want, after I unload my trailer, we could leave and go over the finances."

"And miss the auction?" She looked up at him. "I've never

been to a livestock sale before. I'd like to go."

"Good. I'll be right back." He gave her that smile again, the one that lit his eyes and displayed slightly crooked teeth, and another pancake flipped in her chest.

But he returned later with a set jaw and stormy eyes. When he caught sight of her, he smiled, but not with the warmth he'd had before he left. If Patricia had been watching, maybe she'd have an idea what had changed his mood. But she had felt self-conscious sitting alone in a diner full of ranchers and had gone in search of a ladies' room.

Talon came beside her. "You ready?"

The question hardly sounded like an invitation, and her temper threatened to rise at the tone of his voice. But she nodded. Surely whatever had upset him had nothing to do with her.

With a hand on her back, he guided her past the foyer to a set of stairs covered in a worn red carpet. At the top, a set of glass doors opened into the auditorium. She had expected the place to smell as the pens had outdoors—strong with hay, cow patties, and mud—but the predominant odor was fresh dirt. The air was musty, but not offensive.

Below her, a theater with cushioned seats descended in a semicircle toward the strangest "stage" she had ever seen. Two parallel pipe rails formed an arced runway from a wood-paneled gate on the left to another one on the right. A third gate sat off-center in the middle. The panels on all three were rough and battered, the jagged edges evidence of attacks by frightened animals.

In the runway, a black calf darted from the first gate to the center one while the auctioneer above it called out numbers between hums of gibberish. He barely shouted, "Sold!" before starting his hum for the next calf. The center gateman let the first calf pass through while a new one appeared from the gate on the left. Then, as the first calf ran out the right door, the second was held in its place, and a new one came in on the left. The harried animals were rushed in and out as if riding a conveyor belt.

One calf rammed the center gate and twisted around in the narrow space. The men in the runway jumped behind the protective panels and prodded the animal in the right direction.

Patricia grimaced. "Oh, the poor thing! Doesn't that hurt?"

"About as much as static electricity would hurt you." He pointed to where Chance and Marie were sitting, and they moved toward them.

When they took their seats, Marie leaned to her and nodded toward a big-bellied rancher in a brown felt Stetson. "He's been winning most of the bids."

The rancher's ankle was propped on the opposite leg, and his hand rested on his knee. When the auctioneer hummed his tune for a new calf, the man's index finger flicked up. Farther to his right, another man in a sweat-stained straw hat nodded, and the two silently battled over the calf until the second one yielded.

"Who is that man?" Patricia asked. "Is he the buyer for a restaurant?"

"No, he's just another rancher." Talon said. "Restaurants don't buy from auctions like this one. They go to the rancher—which is why I'd like to upgrade the Circle Bar's herd to Angus."

"That always has been one of Talon's dreams," Chance said. He leaned forward to address Talon on the other side of Marie and Patricia and pointed to his watch. "We've got to get out of here if we're going to ride tonight."

Marie mewed her disappointment, but Patricia was ready to

go. Talon's mood had lightened a bit, but whatever had upset him still hovered in his eyes. "We need to go too. We have to check out of the motel."

Talon raised a brow. "You're not leaving Texas already, are you?"

"No, no–just changing locations."

"Good." Chance stood. "Y'all come to the rodeo tonight. We'll have some guest passes waiting at the ticket booth."

Marie rose also and rubbed his riding arm. "I'll even bring you luck."

Patricia glanced at Talon, but he seemed miles away, perhaps thinking of his ride tonight or whatever had upset him earlier. Under different circumstances, she'd prod gently and get him to confide in her. But in three days, she'd be putting the ranch up for sale and heading back to New York. She shouldn't get close to a cowboy she'd never see again.

Talon pulled his rig onto the blacktop and headed for home. Spending the bulk of the day with his new boss hadn't been as clamp-jawed frustrating as he'd expected. He'd actually enjoyed it, until the other ranchers asked him about her when he went to unload his truck.

Maybe he should've told them who she was, maybe introduce her, but he couldn't get the words out of his mouth. *This is Patricia Talbert, new owner of the Circle Bar.*

Nope. He just couldn't say it. Made it seem too real. He wasn't ready.

But he had liked being with her. She was a beautiful woman– not a sophisticated beauty like Marie, but a girl-next-door kind of beautiful that kept him tongue-tied and wishing they'd had more time together.

His empty trailer bounced over a pothole and jolted the truck. He flicked his eyes to the rearview. Chance swerved around the hole. If Talon had kept his mind on his driving instead of his boss, he would've missed it too. His thoughts hadn't been this occupied with a woman in years, and Patricia Talbert was a bad choice to fill the void.

He didn't need the void filled. The ranch took up his attention. And bull riding. And breeding his horses. And a host of other things. He didn't need a woman on his mind. Particularly not the one who held his future in her hands.

Thirty minutes later, he backed the truck in front of the equipment shed and stepped out, leaving the keys in the ignition. He called Randy and Jack over to clean out the trailer as he strode toward Frank, who rose from a rocker on the bunkhouse porch.

Frank crossed the gravel drive to meet him, his gait stilted by an old rodeo injury. His mustache twitched over a grin. "What'd ya do with the new boss, boy? Scare her off?"

"Naw. She'll be at the rodeo tonight."

"How'd she handle the auction?"

Talon pushed back his hat. "Well, she didn't go all girlie over it, if that's what you mean. She didn't hold her nose or squeak out a series of *ews*. Actually seemed interested."

"Wonder if that means she's going to run the place." Frank hooked his thumbs in his jeans pockets. "Did you ask her what her plans are?"

Talon winced. No. He hadn't.

Frank reached for the cigar he used to keep in his shirt pocket

Give the Lady a Ride

a dozen years ago. Now and then, he still had the hankering for a smoke, still reached to his pocket. His empty hand slid up to his chin and rubbed the stubble. "Well, I reckon we'll find out sooner or later."

Chance pulled in and backed his truck beside Talon's. He sauntered toward them, grinning bigger than Dallas. "Marie's great, isn't she? She's got her own store in Manhattan. Sells high-dollar clothes to rich women. She was a model once, you know that? Magazine cover girl. Yep. She's something."

"Yeah. Something." Frank stepped closer to him. "What did you find out about the boss lady?"

"The boss lady?" Chance couldn't have looked more surprised if Frank had told him he'd sprouted antenna. "I didn't think to ask about her. Besides, she was with Talon . . . "

Chance turned to Talon, who shook his head.

"Sometimes you boys just don't have the sense God gave a bull." Frank scowled from one to the other. "How could y'all spend six hours with that woman and *not* ask what she's going to do with the ranch?"

Talon winced again. What could he say?

Chapter Four

"Score's in for Talon Carlson: Eighty-seven point five. Great ride! Give the cowboy a hand, ladies and gentlemen." The announcer's voice boomed over the loudspeaker.

Talon took a knee for a quick prayer. The Lord had given him a safe ride; thanking Him for a successful one was always a bonus. With the roar of the crowd ringing in his ears, he rose and headed back to the locker room. Fellow rodeo contestants lining the alleyway slapped his back and congratulated him as he passed. He dipped his head and grinned.

Chance would be up after the rider currently taking his turn on the sand. Talon switched course and walked down the back of the bucking chutes to join him.

He excused himself past the crew and the back judge, who watched for rule-compliance from behind the chute, just as Chance slid onto his bull. "Get 'er done."

Chance wrapped his riding hand in the bull rope and flicked him a glance. "Did you see her?"

"Who?"

"Marie." He readjusted the rope and pulled it snug again.

"She's up front, to the left of the center post."

Talon frowned. "Chance, you'd better keep your mind on your ride. Focus, man, focus!"

Chance gave a sharp nod. With Talon at the ready to catch his vest should the bull buck, he wriggled up Razin' Cane's red back and adjusted his hand in the rope one more time. When he was situated at the bull's shoulders, he raised his free hand and yelled at the gateman.

"Pull it!"

Razin' rocketed from the chute and charged several yards into the arena before starting a bucking spin to the right–into Chance's riding hand. Chance rode high on Razin's back and kept the bull's easy rhythm: duck head, sling flank; duck head, sling flank. But then the bull tightened the spin like a dog chasing his tail, ducking and slinging faster with each round. Chance tilted; the bull's momentum began pulling him into the vortex of the spin.

Talon's thigh muscles tensed and his riding hand flexed, as if through remote control he could yank Chance from the well. The eight-second horn sounded an instant before Chance's left leg slipped off the bull. Grinning, Talon popped a fist on the chute rail and waited for Chance to jump up and perform his customary victory move–the belly bump with the bullfighters.

But Chance's hand didn't come free. It was hung in the rope. He fell inside the spin, his back against the right shoulder of the still-bucking bull, and his right arm extended above him. The bullfighters charged in and tried to free him while the bull yanked him around like a marionette. His free arm waved a furious farewell as each buck jerked him off his feet.

When his riding hand broke free, Chance fell in a heap. One

of the fighters slapped the bull's neck and drew him away, while the other helped Chance to his feet. Talon had been holding his breath until his friend headed to the chutes. But Chance turned and went back toward the spectators. With his left hand, he flung his hat into the stands, then grabbed his right arm, pain twisting his features, and strode from the arena.

Talon looked in the direction of the toss. Marie clutched Chance's hat to her chest. From just a few rows away, he could see the concern on her face.

"They are absolutely crazy and I don't mind saying so." Marie *had* said so at least fifteen times. "Absolutely crazy!"

"No argument here." Patricia struggled to keep up with Marie's longer strides. They raced down the corridor toward the sports doctor's exam station, a section separated from the rest of the locker room with a heavy tan canvas. Like one of the bulls the men rode, Marie barreled through clusters of cowboys who warned her that spectators weren't allowed in back of the chutes.

Once they found the entrance to the exam room, Marie came to such an abrupt halt, Patricia almost rammed into her. Inside, Chance slumped, tight-lipped and pale, on a white-sheeted gurney, his shirt off and his right shoulder wrapped under an ice bag.

When he saw Marie, he straightened and puffed out his smooth, muscular chest. "Hey, pretty lady. Did you catch my hat?"

Marie melted before Patricia's eyes. The steam she'd built up evaporated, and she stared at the black felt hat in her hand as if seeing it for the first time. She stepped into the room just far enough to stretch her arm out and give it to him.

"Thank you, ma'am." Chance's eyes were as gray as the Atlantic in a Nor'easter, and Marie flushed when he winked one at her.

Her lip quivered as she studied his wrapped shoulder.

From the corner, Talon cleared his throat. "He'll be all right, Marie. He just dislocated his shoulder."

"Dislocated his shoulder? He *just* dislocated his shoulder? Are you *nuts*?" She reduced the gap between them in two livid steps and glared at him eye to eye. "It's not like he scratched his finger or stubbed his toe. He *dislocated* his shoulder!"

Talon's lips twitched into a lopsided grin. "Yes, ma'am. And he'll be back on a bull tomorrow."

Another cowboy excused himself and slipped past Patricia into the room. Talon jabbed a thumb at him. "Ask Doc Malone there. He'll tell you if Chance can ride again."

Marie gaped at the six-foot man in Wranglers and black western hat. "You're not the doctor. Tell me you're not the doctor."

"Can't do that, ma'am. It'd be a lie." Dr. Malone wore the same kind of halfway grin most cowboys seem to slap on their faces, but his dark green eyes softened when he spoke. "He'll have a hard time of it, I agree. But he probably will ride again tomorrow night."

"Of course I will." Chance raised his chin a notch. "I'll be fine."

With her lips parted in surprise, Marie swiveled her head from one cowboy to the other. "You guys are insane." She turned wild eyes on Patricia. "Tell them! Tell them they're all insane!"

Give the Lady a Ride

"You're all insane." Her deadpan tone drew a chuckle from the men. She grabbed Marie's wrist and pulled. "Let's get out of here so they can do whatever it is they need to do."

As soon as they were out of earshot, Patricia hissed, "What has gotten into you?"

"I don't know." Marie's eyes misted, her lips scrunched in a losing battle against a frown.

Gripping her shoulders, Patricia glared into her face. "You just met the man. You don't know him well enough to shed a tear over him, not after just a few hours at an auction. Whatever this is, snap out of it!"

Marie sniffed, wiped a knuckle under each eye, and sniffed again.

"We're leaving Tuesday." She'd said those words so often, they'd become her mantra. "There's no such thing as love at first sight, Marie. Get over it."

"You're right." Marie gave a final sniff and straightened her spine. "I'm okay. I'm fine."

"You'd better be." Scowling, Patricia turned and marched out to the parking lot.

"It's a shame, though. He's cute."

"You think Talon's cute too."

"Well, don't you think so?"

"He's not bad." Patricia poked the remote on her key chain and unlocked the Mercedes. "He's just too fond of the word *ma'am*."

Marie approached the car from the passenger side. "Uh-oh. We've got a flat."

Patricia joined her and shook her head. "Do you know how to change a tire?"

"I barely know how to drive. What'll we do now?"

"What's going on over there?" Chance used his left arm to fling his riggin' sack into the back of Talon's pickup.

Talon turned to see Patricia and Marie under a mercury light, crouching beside their car. "Best go see if they need us."

Chance was gone before he got the words out.

Talon shook his head, dropped his bag into the truck bed, and jogged to catch up.

"Need some help?" Chance asked.

Patricia stood. "We have a flat."

"If you'd pop the trunk, we can take a look at the spare." Talon circled to the back of the car.

They unloaded the luggage in the back and found the spare—also flat.

A frown creased Patricia's forehead. "I won't be renting a car from that place again."

"Only one thing to do," Chance said. "Lock up the car and come back with us."

Talon shrugged a shoulder. "You can stay in the ranch house. It's yours anyway."

"That's an idea." Marie beamed, apparently liking the idea of being in such close proximity to Chance. She nudged Patricia. "Want to stay at the ranch?"

"Maybe they should just take us to our motel."

"Which one? The one we just checked out of, or the one in Stephenville we never made reservations for?"

Patricia turned to Talon. "Will we be putting anyone out?"

"No, ma'am. The men stay in the bunkhouse. The main house is empty at night."

Give the Lady a Ride

Marie rested a hand on her arm. "Let's just ride with them. We can get the car in the morning."

"I guess we can." Patricia rubbed her temples. "I don't see that we have much of a choice."

"Now you're talking." Chance wasted no time pulling up the rod on a rolling suitcase and herding the women to the truck.

"We won't all have to squeeze into the front, will we?" Patricia asked him as they crossed the parking area.

"Oh, no ma'am," Chance said. "We've got a four-door cab . . ."

Talon stayed with the suitcases scattered behind the car while their laughter drifted back to him. How convenient for Chance to be injured. He repositioned the spare and closed the trunk, then loaded his arms with flowery bags and cosmetic kits that smelled like some fu-fu store, and trudged to the pickup like a pack mule.

By the time Talon reached the truck, Chance had the ladies' full attention while he recounted his ride. Marie sat beside him in the backseat of the extended cab and seemed to hang onto his every word. Facing them from the front passenger seat, Patricia gnawed on her bottom lip and seemed just as enthralled.

". . . you're supposed to hug the bull's neck when you're hung like that. Keeps you from slipping under him or getting gored," Chance said. "But the way I fell and the way he kept buckin' and spinnin', I just couldn't flip around to grab hold. It was all I could do to keep my feet under me every time he kicked."

"Doesn't your arm hurt?" Marie's voice dripped with sympathy and awe, as if Chance had injured himself parting the Red Sea.

"Just a bit, ma'am."

Talon snorted and settled a suitcase in the truck bed. Truth be known, a dislocated shoulder hurt like the dickens, and the pain eased only slightly once the joint was back in place. Doc had iced his shoulder, given him some Tylenol–Chance refused anything stronger–and sent him on his way. Those two tablets would dull the pain for a while, but he'd be rummaging through the medicine cabinet tonight.

Talon listened to the *Poor Chance!* show emanating from the cab as he unloaded the rest of his burden into the truck. He grabbed a blue tarp from the toolbox and pulled it over everything, then secured it with bungee cords. Jerking the keys from his pocket, he took a deep breath, knocking the perfume smells from his nose with the odors of hay, dirt, and livestock.

His gut twisted painfully at the changes he had to face. He missed Jake like he'd missed his own father when he died, and hadn't stopped missing Loretta even though she'd passed several years ago. His future seemed uncertain, and bringing the new boss to the ranch just drove home that point. To top it off, he found her attractive–a dangerous thing to a man who was destined to be single.

Lord, give me strength.

Twenty minutes into the drive, Chance and Marie were murmuring to each other in the back, and Patricia still couldn't convince herself to strike up a conversation with Talon. With her arms crossed, she faced the passenger window, though she saw little in the darkness. She was aggravated and couldn't decide which irked her the worst, Marie's senseless reaction to Chance's injury, or the fact that Chance and Talon would subject themselves to such injuries.

Talon cranked up the sound on his CD player. Since he hadn't tried to talk to her, Patricia assumed he wasn't any more interested in chatter than she was. She closed her eyes for a few moments and listened to the music, but her mind wouldn't drift away from the questions burning to be asked.

She turned the volume down and twisted in her seat to face him. "What on earth makes you climb onto the back of a bull? Competitiveness? Macho pride? Is it the danger? Is that why you and Chance risk your lives?"

"I guess so, to a certain extent. There's nothing quite like bull riding."

"Anything for a thrill," she snapped, and shook her head. "What is it? Do you feel you have to prove how tough you are? That's just crazy! Instead of that dislocated shoulder, Chance could've been killed tonight. *You* could've been killed last night!"

"Could've been, but we weren't."

"Not this time. But it's an insane risk. And for what? Rodeos stem from ranch work, and I really don't think riding a bull is a necessary chore of ranching. I think you two are just a couple of Neanderthals flexing your muscles for all the other Neanderthals out there. All brawn and no brain."

The sudden silence in the cab sparked with electricity. The hair on the nape of her neck prickled as she felt everyone's eyes boring into her. Even though it was how she felt at the moment, she couldn't believe she'd just called her hosts Neanderthals. Had she left all her diplomacy in New York? "I'm sorry. Really. I didn't mean to say that."

Talon's laughter diffused the tension. "You're not too far wrong. There is definitely a macho element to bull riding. It's a tough sport that attracts tough men."

"I guess I just don't understand." Patricia settled back in her seat and sighed. "Why would you climb on the back of a bull?"

Talon looked at her, his features softly colored by the dashboard lights. "What is it you love? What gives you the greatest challenge and sense of accomplishment when you succeed? What drives you, makes your adrenaline rush?"

Patricia clasped her hands in her lap. How could she answer him? What gave her satisfaction, a sense of accomplishment? Getting a taxi in rush hour? Juggling the demands on her father's time?

"I don't know," she whispered. "I really don't know what gives me an adrenaline rush. Definitely nothing like what you do. Nothing that compares to bull riding."

"Yes, ma'am, that's the point." He stopped at a blinking red light in a sleepy town, then turned right for the final leg of the trip. "Bull riding is a high form of athleticism. You match your abilities, your strength, your concentration to an animal that outweighs you by over a thousand pounds. Taking the risk, making the eight. There's nothing like it."

"And if you don't make the eight?"

"There's always next time."

Patricia studied his profile as his words washed over her. *Always next time.* He held a strong faith that he would have a next time.

Give the Lady a Ride

Chapter Five

At four in the morning, Patricia gave up trying to sleep. She changed into a pair of shorts and a t-shirt, and felt her way in the dark to the kitchen downstairs in search of coffee. Back home, she'd watched Melba make it; it couldn't be that hard to do. She went through the cabinets until she found everything and assembled it in front of the coffee maker. After filling the carafe halfway with tap water and pouring it into the coffee maker, she dumped several tablespoons of Folgers into the filter and flicked the machine on. Nothing to do now but wait. She pulled out a red vinyl chair from the small breakfast table in the center of the room and settled in.

Talon's questions from last night had grated her like a windblown tree branch scratching across the window screen. Since she'd found out the truth about Kent, nothing excited her, nothing caused the adrenaline to pump through her veins. Her life centered around her work and occasional outings with people whose motives for her friendship were continually suspect.

Her work for her father provided some satisfaction. Each

successful fundraiser she planned helped him with his campaign. She believed in the senator; his goals were her goals. Keeping him in office mattered to her. She played a role, small but important, and possessed a sense of accomplishment in that.

But the thing which brought her that sense of accomplishment was the very thing she hated about her life. Politicians attracted the ambitious like a news crew to scandal, and her father was no different. Being the gateway to his presence had brought her more than her share of heartache. Marie was the only friend she could trust.

What would it be like to have a new start in a place where no one knew her father or cared about his position–a place so far west she could leave the memories of her miserable marriage behind? How exciting it would be to hit "refresh" or "escape," as she did on her computer, and simply begin a new life here in Texas.

But could she live on a ranch? Be the employer of a man like Talon?

She grabbed the saltshaker off the table and rolled it between her hands, hearing the soft *click-click* as it tapped her rings. Why was she even thinking about living on the ranch? This was an election year. Everything would be crazy for the next six months, and her assistant might not be able to handle it alone. Patricia had a responsibility to her father which she couldn't just dump on Marcy. Finishing her business here and getting back to work should be foremost in her mind.

The coffee maker gurgled and hissed out its final drops. She poured a cup, added a little sugar and a touch of cream, and wandered through the dining room. The sturdy table could seat eight as easily as any formal dining set, but instead of the sheen of a mahogany finish, it held the dull yellow of old pine. Instead of elegant cushioned seats, hard benches stood askew on either side of the table, and mismatched chairs snuggled against its ends. Ranch life would be so different from what she was used to.

She slipped out the back door. The fresh night air caressed her, sweeter than she'd ever smelled in Manhattan. She would love waking up to these scents and this peaceful hush which was so elusive back home. Leaning forward against the rail, she looked out from under the eaves to see the star-draped sky. Stars like these shunned New York, and city lights couldn't compare.

She followed the veranda around the house until she could see the moon and the pale yellow light it cast across the hills. A soft halo circled the moon. The ring was a sign for something, wasn't it? Rain? Or was it heat?

"Good evening." Talon's baritone voice startled her.

She turned and smiled at his dark shape on the first step. "I think it's morning now. What are you doing up this early?"

"Couldn't sleep. Everyone's going to be up in an hour anyway. What about you?"

"Same. I made coffee. You want a cup?" The brew had been so easy to make, she felt confident offering him some.

He followed her around the house, then reached past her to open the back door and allow her through. She warmed at the gesture. It was a simple courtesy he'd performed more than once, but in the intimacy of the pre-dawn, it made her feel special.

"I'm surprised the kitchen is so well stocked. Even the cream is fresh." She filled a mug and handed it to him. "Has someone been using the house?"

Talon grimaced at his first sip. He frowned and set the mug

down. The coffee was probably too hot. She hadn't ventured a taste of hers yet for that very reason.

"We have our meals here. Chef and Consuela keep the place clean and cook for the men."

"Chef? You have a chef here?"

He laughed and leaned against the counter, crossing his ankles. "No, that's just what Jorge likes to call himself. He thinks it sounds more important than *Cookie*."

She squelched her disappointment and sipped from her mug–and winced. It was strong enough to tap dance across the table and bow through endless curtain calls. Talon's lips held a touch of amusement, and her cheeks grew hot under his gaze.

She pushed her mug aside and cleared her throat. "How many people work on the ranch?"

"It's a busy time right now, so there's six of us. Eight, counting Chef and Consuela. But just Frank, Buster, Chance, and I live in the bunkhouse." He shoved away from the counter and drained his mug in the sink. "We have a few hours before church. You awake enough to go through the books now?"

"Sure." Patricia left her coffee sitting on the table and followed him to the office across the hall. Did he expect her to go to church? She hadn't been since she was child. That he would go incited her curiosity as much as his prayer after his rides. Talon was a bull rider, a ranch foreman, a man's man. He didn't fit the profile of a meek and mild Christian.

But the way he'd apologized for his behavior when she hadn't even thought to take offense, the way he laughed away her insult when she called him a Neanderthal–these seemed to be the actions of a true Christian.

Give the Lady a Ride

In Jake's office, Patricia sat at the scarred desk with a well-worn stock ledger open in front of her. Her hair shone in the light, tempting Talon to run his fingers through it, inviting him for the moment to forget she couldn't make coffee. He leaned over her shoulder to see where she'd stopped in the ledger and caught a faint whiff of her spicy perfume. The scent suited her. Even though she had a girl-next-door appeal, her personality was more complex. She was both shy and confident. She could be as cute as a curious kitten one moment, and all claws and hisses the next. No flower or fruit scent would work for her. She was all spice.

"How big is the ranch?" Her professional tone reminded him to keep his head on straight.

He moved to the other side of the desk, away from her scent and the silky lure of her hair. "Fifteen hundred acres. Small, for Texas."

She pointed at the book. "But this shows you have less than six hundred cows. Is that the maximum capacity for the land?"

"Not in the spring. We can usually handle more this time of year. That's why we didn't cull as many calves as we will later on, when summer starts killing off the hay."

"So you would have to alter your head-to-acre ratio." She tilted her head. "What breed of cattle are you raising?"

"A mix. Some Herefords, Limousine, Charolais, all crossbred. Loretta liked to see the different colors in the herd, so Jake bought some of everything. They're all good breeds and there's health benefits in each, but we're not specialized."

"I'm not sure that makes good business sense." The desk chair squealed as Patricia leaned back. "Didn't Chance say yesterday that you're planning to convert the herd to Angus?"

Talon sucked in his breath and turned his head. Yes. That had been his plan for the Circle Bar when he thought he'd be the owner. Finding out Jake had kin had pulled him into a spin and sent his dreams for the place into the vortex. Jake had left him solely responsible for the ranch until the new owner showed up, but that hadn't given him a blank check to change the way it was run. "I'm not sure what we're going to do yet, ma'am. That's your call."

"Makes sense to me. Aren't you in the business of raising beef cattle? Isn't Angus one of the best beef breeds?"

"Yes, ma'am." Hope leapt like a bull from the chute. She agreed the herd should be changed. Would she agree to the other changes he wanted to make?

He couldn't sit still. "Sun's up. Would you like to see the spread? We could take the horses out and ride. You'll see what you've got here."

She bit her lip. "I don't have any riding outfits."

"If you're not too picky, I'll see what I can do."

Her eyes lit, and her lips curled into a smile she seemed barely able to contain. "I'm not picky at all."

"Good deal." He slapped the desk. "Be right back."

He left the house and crossed the gravel drive. Patricia seemed to know far more about ranching than he had given her credit for. Would she be interested in his ideas? Being foreman of a ranch whose stock he controlled was almost as good as owning it himself. *Almost.*

Lights glowed from the bunkhouse windows. He pushed open the door and strode inside. The men, who were getting ready for morning chores, turned to look at him. The blessed scent of coffee wafted to him from the machine in the corner, and he couldn't get to it fast enough.

Chance tapped his razor against the sink, eyeing Talon through the open bathroom door. "Where've ya been?"

"Talking with the new owner." He filled a mug, downed a quarter of the brew, then leaned back against the table to talk to Chance's reflection. "You should hear some of the questions she's asking. We may have ourselves a real boss after all. Get this." He gestured toward the main house with his coffee mug. "She thinks we should have Angus cattle on the spread."

Buster sat on his bunk and jerked a boot on. "Sure don't sound like she's gonna sell, does it? Turnin' a herd takes time." He planted his hands on his knees. "You tell her that's what you been wantin'?"

"Chance told her yesterday." Talon sipped his coffee and looked the men over. At five feet, seven inches, and a hundred sixty pounds, Frank was the smallest one there. "Frank, you got a clean pair of jeans?"

"Yeah, why?"

"Let me have 'em, okay? And I need Sable and Tandy saddled and ready to ride in twenty minutes." He put his half-empty mug down and grinned. "The lady boss wants to see her new ranch."

"Good sign." Frank tossed his britches to Talon.

"Mighty good sign."

The jeans were too long, too tight in the hips, and too loose in the waist, but Patricia did her best to make them fit, cuffing the hems and cinching the waist with a leather belt from a skirt she'd packed. She hadn't thought to bring her riding boots, so her casual loafers would have to do.

Sitting in Uncle Jake's office and reading the stock ledger seemed to have awakened a long-dormant part of her memory. When she was young, years before her father became a senator, he'd tell her bedtime stories about the big ranch in Texas, about summers so hot the grass would die and the streams would dry to a trickle, and about early mornings on horseback, rounding up a herd to auction off before cattle prices bottomed out. Looking back now made her smile. Most little girls dreamed of fairytale castles and princes on white horses. She'd slept with cattle-drive images derived from her father's stories and old John Wayne movies.

While she couldn't claim to know all the ins and outs of ranching, at least she hadn't looked like an idiot in front of Talon.

She raced downstairs and through the screen door, heading to the stable gate where Talon sat astride a snorting black mare. In his right hand, he held the reins to a gentle-eyed dappled gray gelding no taller than fifteen hands. When she was younger, she had ridden champion show horses, competing in the jumping arena until she graduated from Vanderbilt. She couldn't wait to climb on the gray's back.

Chance stood near the barn with a couple of cowboys she had yet to meet. They feigned busyness, eyeing her surreptitiously as if ready for a good show from the city girl, but not ready to get caught anticipating it.

Talon extended the gelding's reins toward her. "His name's Tandy. He's the easiest ride we have up here. You'll get used to him before you know it. Just grab hold of the horn and the back of the saddle, put your left foot in the stirrup, and swing your right leg over. Nothing to it."

She bit back a grin and snatched Tandy's reins from Talon's grip, then easily swung into the saddle. "Like that?"

With a gleam of approval in his eyes, Talon touched the brim of his hat in salute. "Yes, ma'am."

He clicked to his horse, turned away from the stables and the cattle pens, and followed a path to the edge of the plateau where the main and bunk houses and the outbuildings stood. When he pulled rein, he swept a hand toward the land below. "Welcome to the Circle Bar."

Meandering streams crisscrossed a verdant valley. Trees stippled the hills, sporting their new green coats in the early morning sun. The land rolled gently under dew-kissed grass and yellow wild flowers. Prickly pear cactus and out-croppings of rocks dotted the pastures.

"Most of the ranch is in a basin," Talon said. "The hills form a horseshoe around it."

Fences, barely visible in the distance, divided the land into four pastures, not including the small one behind the horse barn. Each pasture held its own large pond and a peppering of live oaks, cedars, and squatty trees Talon called mesquite. He pointed to a long, open shed covering massive, round hay bales. "God willing, we'll have that filled up to take us through the dry season and into the winter."

He touched his heels to his horse's sides, resuming the slow walk down the hill. Patricia kept a light hold on the reins so Tandy could pick his way. The cattle looked up from their grazing and lumbered off as the riders reached the bottom of the hill.

Ahead, just left of the trail, a calf nuzzled his mother's flank.

Another scampered in the field, and another fed. Acres of cattle—black, red, brown, white—spread before her in the front pasture, and for almost every cow, there was a hungry calf. The sight filled her with the joy of new life.

Regardless of the premium beef breed, she could see why Aunt Loretta had wanted a variety in the pastures. The different colors appealed to Patricia too. But converting to Angus was a good business decision, and Talon would be wise to do it. Regret niggled at her. By the time the land was black with Angus calves, she would no longer be the owner. She sighed. "They're so cute."

"You seem to belong right here on the ranch with them." Talon dipped his head, then twisted it to look at her. "You know more about ranching than I gave you credit for. Can I ask what your plans are?"

Patricia's stomach knotted. She was enjoying the ride and his company, but his mood was sure to change the minute she said she planned to sell the ranch. As excited as he was about changing the herd over, it would crush him to realize it wouldn't be his decision to make. The new owner may like the color mix just fine. "Right now, I'd keep all the land in Texas if—"

Talon's horse spooked to the side, his head up, eyes wide. Patricia caught a glimpse of a large gray rabbit dashing away just as her horse jerked hard right and bolted through the herd.

Give the Lady a Ride

Chapter Six

Patricia pulled back on the reins, but Tandy stretched his neck and raced to the low sweeping branches of a stand of live oaks. She leaned low over his neck, with the saddle horn digging into her stomach, as he skirted the limbs. Twigs scraped her and threatened to tear through her clothes and into her flesh. Horse and rider broke past the tree line and streaked through a clearing. Cactus and brush whizzed by as Tandy shot to the other end of the pasture.

Her breath caught in her chest at the sight of a barbed-wire fence just a few strides ahead. Tandy flew over it, and she held on for the ride. When her mount landed, she shoved herself upright in the saddle.

"Whoa! Whoa, boy!" She leaned back, pushing her feet against the stirrups and pulling the reins with both hands. "Whoa!"

Tandy slid on his haunches and danced to a stop. His body heaved beneath her as he sucked air into his lungs.

"Are you all right?" Talon shouted. He reined to halt beside her and dismounted before she had the breath to answer. "Are you okay?"

"I'm fine." But like Tandy, her lungs hungered for the sweet air. She managed a smile between gasps. "That was exhilarating."

"*Exhilarating*? You had me scared to death!" He reached up, wrapped strong hands around her waist and pulled her off the horse.

When her feet hit the ground, she kept her grasp on his muscled forearms for support. With her legs as wobbly as Silly String and her pulse thundering in her ears, his steady strength was a comfort.

But the sudden warmth coursing through her body wasn't.

She released him and backed away, raising a shaky hand to her hair, and offered him a sheepish smile. "I haven't ridden like that in years."

Talon hated to let go and fought the urge to crush her in his arms. "Are you sure you're okay?"

"Yes, I'm fine." Her smile wavered.

"I didn't know Tandy would charge off like that. I'm really sorry, ma'am."

She shot him a look of exasperation. "You don't have to call me *ma'am* all the time. I told you to call me Patricia."

He stifled a grin. Texas etiquette sure didn't sit well with her. "Not 'Pat'?"

She touched a finger to her chin, and a smile twitched her lips. "That would fit better out here, wouldn't it?"

"Yes, ma'am."

"*Pat.*" Her scowl was undermined by the humor in her eyes.

"Pat."

The horses drifted away, finding new grass to munch. Talon and Pat ambled along behind them.

Give the Lady a Ride

"You're just full of surprises. You know about ranching. And you can ride far better than you can make coffee." He flicked her a grin. "You've ridden before?"

"A bit. Junior champion show jumper three years in a row."

"Wow." He hadn't figured her for a horsewoman. He reached for Sable's bridle and turned the horse back the way they came. "Do you still ride?"

"Not since college. Don't have the time." She took Tandy's reins and held them loosely as she walked to Talon's side. The horse followed her like a docile puppy. "I'm my dad's social coordinator. He's a U.S. Senator."

"From Texas?"

"No, New York."

"I thought you said he was from around here."

"He was, but he hated ranching. When he graduated college, he landed a job with a Dallas firm that had a home base in New York. He was transferred up there, met my mom and, well, the rest is history. We only came back here that once."

"Guess it seemed like a different world to a ten-year-old."

"Still does."

He found a pebble in the grass and flung it. It clattered against a nearby collection of smooth-surfaced stones in a dry creek bed. "You said Jake and your father were brothers? Why isn't your name McAllister?"

"Talbert was my husband's name." She looked away. "I kept it to maintain a professional distance between my father and me."

He slipped her a glance. "Talbert *was* your husband's name. You're divorced?"

"Widowed."

59

"Sorry to hear that." He cringed. The woman's marital status was her own affair. He had no business asking. But he couldn't deny the relief he felt that she wasn't married.

"What about you?" She shoulder-nudged him. "Have you ever been married?"

Her question was what he got for being nosy, and he was obliged to answer. "Came close once."

She looked at him as if she expected more, but he'd told her all he was going to for now. He chucked another rock.

She flicked Tandy's reins against her hand. "So how did you meet Jake and Loretta?"

"They took me in after my folks died."

"Sorry about your parents. How did they die?"

"House fire. Had something to do with the Christmas lights– bare wire or something."

"That's awful. I'm so sorry." A cool morning breeze lifted her hair and blew it across her cheek. He wanted to reach out and brush it aside.

"Thanks." He shoved his free hand in his pocket and shifted his gaze to the distant hill, away from her sympathetic eyes and soft blonde hair. "Jake and Loretta took me in and raised me as their own. Not long after, Chance's parents died in a car accident, and I had myself a kid brother."

"So they took you both in?"

"They were childless and big-hearted. You would've liked them."

"They seemed nice, from what I can remember. How old were you when you came?"

"Sixteen."

"Did you start bull riding then?"

Give the Lady a Ride

"Yeah, got a late start." He grinned at the surprise in her eyes. "Chance's folks worked on this ranch. Jake had him riding when he was seven."

She squinted at him. "They put a seven-year-old on a bull?"

"A tame one. That's the way kids learn. Buster started about that age. Old Frank was bustin' broncs by twelve. He's got more silver buckles than anyone I know." He reached for a blade of grass and stuck it between his teeth. "How old were you when you started riding?"

"Seven." She laughed. "It just seems different to put a seven-year-old on a kid-friendly horse than to put him on the back of a bull."

"Aw, it wasn't a big bull." Sable snorted and nudged him from behind. "Looks like she's ready to run again. You game?"

"I'll race you back to the house." Pat swung into Tandy's saddle and was kicking flank before he had a foot in the stirrup.

He jumped aboard Sable. "You're gonna lose!"

Chapter Seven

"Y ou should've seen her." Talon dug a serving spoon into the scrambled eggs, then passed the bowl to Chance on his right. "She rode like a pro."

Patricia squirmed on the hard bench, but couldn't help grinning. Although she'd lost the race back to the house by a nose, it had felt so good to ride again. Her morning with Talon was refreshing–just what she needed after too many years in a business suit.

Marie, Chance, and the two ranch hands she'd just met, Frank Simmons and Buster Milligan, smiled at her as if she were a hero. The way Talon bragged about her made her sound like one.

Frank leaned around Marie to look at Patricia. "I've never known Tandy to be so skittish."

"But I have known him to run his rider under a branch." Across from her, Buster shoveled eggs onto his plate and reached for the bacon. "You got off lucky."

"Pure skill." Talon winked at her, then turned to Chance. "Did you see about the car?"

"Sent Jack and Randy." Chance's eyes shifted from his plate to Marie. "Besides, I had something else I wanted to do."

A pretty shade of pink flushed Marie's cheeks. At eight in the morning, she was rarely awake. Now, here she was, not only awake and dressed, but blushing. Marie *never* blushed. Patricia raised a questioning brow at her, but received only a shrug in response.

She'd have to get the scoop later–she was famished. With an enthusiasm matching any hand on the ranch, she dove into the bacon and eggs. Talon passed a bowl of what must've been "grits" to her; she spooned up a serving and plopped some butter in, just as the men had done. The hominy dish wasn't unknown in New York, but she'd never tried it. She swirled the melting butter around and loaded a spoonful of the steaming cereal.

Chance wiped his mouth with a paper napkin. "If you don't mind my asking, ma'am, what are you planning to do with the ranch?"

Everyone's eyes turned to her, and her shoulders knotted. The expectation on their faces soured her stomach with guilt, and she lowered her spoon. She couldn't escape the question now.

Marie was no help. The same hopeful look the men wore was reflected in her eyes, as if she too wanted Patricia to keep the ranch. Whatever had been cooking between her and Chance since the auction had steamed Marie's brain. Patricia could not stay in Texas and become a rancher. It was out of the question.

Wasn't it?

She slipped her lip between her teeth. The idea of starting life anew here was tempting, but it would be a huge step. Massive. And she wasn't sure she could do it. Besides, she loved New

Give the Lady a Ride

York. She loved her apartment in Manhattan, the shopping, restaurants, and theaters.

On the other hand, she'd like to give herself more time here. After the ride, she could feel the love of this land squirming its way into her heart. Here, she could escape the things she detested about her life in New York.

Her hand fisted around the napkin in her lap. She had no time for daydreams. Before she'd left New York, she had decided to sell the ranch. She had to. With her father's campaign in full swing, she couldn't afford to dally with thoughts of starting life over. She should do what she came to do and get back to work.

Taking a deep breath, she forced herself to meet Chance's eyes. "I have an appointment with a real estate agent in the morning."

Nothing back home could match the sudden silence at the table. The tightness in her shoulders spread down her back as her eyes slid from face to face. Chance shook his bowed head. Frank stroked his mustache and stared out the window. Buster's bushy brows knit between his downcast eyes.

"Well, that's a shame, ma'am." Talon wadded up his napkin and chucked it onto his plate. "A real shame."

He stood and left the room in two strides. Her body jerked at the slam of the back door.

"It's your ranch, ma'am. I reckon you'll do what you need to do." Frank rose from the bench. "If you'll excuse me, I've got to get back to work."

Chance and Buster left their unfinished breakfast on the table and drifted from the room without so much as a glance in her direction.

"I wish you'd reconsider." Marie whispered.

"We've talked about this." Patricia's voice was harsh, but she didn't care. She needed Marie's support, but now that her friend had found a new man to toy with, her mind would be mush for awhile. "It makes no sense to keep the ranch. I can't run it from New York, and I'm not going to move here. I have responsibilities at home." She pushed her plate away. "So do you."

"There has to be a way, Pattie. It's so beautiful out here; I'd hate to see you get rid of it."

"You're certainly singing a new tune! You weren't one bit impressed with Texas until you spent the day with Chance yesterday." Patricia tilted her head. "And just what was that little exchange between you two this morning? I don't believe I've *ever* seen you blush before. What did you do?"

"Nothing!"

Patricia leaned closer. "Tell the truth."

"Honest, Pattie." Marie avoided her gaze. "He knocked on the front door around seven-thirty this morning—"

"It takes more than a knock to wake you up."

"Okay, he *pounded* on the door. Is that better?" Marie glared. "Anyway, he said you and Talon had already gone riding and asked if I would like to go riding too."

A horse hair could've knocked Patricia over. "You don't know how to ride."

"I know, I told him. He wants to teach me." She looked at Patricia from the corner of her eye. "If we stay long enough for me to learn."

"We're not staying long enough . . . Wait a minute. That little invitation isn't what made you blush." Patricia leaned on her elbow. "Okay. Give."

"It's nothing. Really. We just went to the barn and let the

horses loose into the pasture, then we walked around a little."

"And?"

"And, nothing." She huffed. "He's just different, that's all. He has a way about him that's unlike anyone I've ever met. I really like him."

Patricia slapped the table. "I knew it! You just want to add to your list of admirers."

"No! It's not like that!"

She shot a finger toward Marie. "You can't leave your store, and I can't leave Dad's campaign. We have work to do! Come Tuesday, we will be on that plane."

She was going to sell his home. Pain gripped Talon's heart, the same kind of pain he'd felt whenever he lost someone he loved. Now he was losing some*thing.*

What can I do about it, Lord?

He couldn't buy it from her. His income, even if combined with Chance's, wouldn't be enough to pay off the mortgage on a ranch this size.

What was he thinking? His income *came* from this ranch. If it was sold, he may not have a job, much less an income, unless the new owner kept him on.

He dumped a scoop of oats into a bucket, grabbed the antibiotic salve and some clean bandages from the tack room, and headed for Bodine's stall. With a snort, the horse stretched his neck toward the bucket. The buckskin's gentle brown eyes and the shape of his head were evidence of the touch of Arabian blood in his heritage. To Talon, he was the best-looking animal on the ranch.

"Hello, buddy. Feeling better?" He rubbed Bodine's neck while the horse munched the oats. After a bit, Talon slipped a halter over the horse's head, led him out to the back of the stables and tied the lead rope to a post.

"One thing's for sure, boy, you belong to me. If I have to go, you're going with me."

He didn't own much: a couple of silver buckles, his pickup, Oz, his border collie, and Bodine and Sable, his cutting horses. Not much to show for thirty-six years of life. He used to count his home here as a possession, but his future on the ranch now rested in the hands of someone he barely knew. And the Lord's hands. Jake and Loretta had taught him to leave his problems at God's throne, a lesson that had proven itself well worth learning. But Talon hadn't mastered the second half of it yet: Don't worry.

Bodine's withers twitched as Talon unwrapped the old dressing. Although the horse still limped, the wound showed signs of healing. Pink flesh circled the once-infected gouge in the middle. Talon got the hose, turned the water to a trickle, and returned to wash the leg.

If the ranch sold, Buster and the younger men would be okay. They'd find other jobs if they had to. Chef and Consuela, though in their fifties, could still find work. But Frank was the oldest one here. Had he saved enough to retire?

Maybe Talon and Chance should stop the smaller rodeos and get their professional membership cards. Take it to the pros, get on the circuit. Give the current bull riding champ a run for his money.

The thought held no appeal. Riding was just for fun; he was a rancher first. If he couldn't work this ranch, he'd move on to the next one. He'd have to buy a horse trailer. A small one, just big enough for his two mounts. Chance would need a trailer too.

"We wouldn't want him to leave Millie behind, would we, boy?" He tossed the hose aside and twisted the top of the salve jar.

Bodine had paired with Millie to produce some good cutting horses, which had helped pad the two men's pockets. A couple of the mares he'd sired were still here on the ranch, property of the Circle Bar.

Talon wrapped a fresh bandage over the wound and patted the horse's shoulder. "There ya go, boy."

He scooped the last of the feed from the bucket and extended his palm. Bodine's soft lips lapped up his reward for being a good patient.

Talon looked over the horse's neck to the field beyond. Tandy and Sable grazed side by side among the other mounts, no worse for wear after their adventure this morning. Talon's eyes swept over the spread. With all his memories and plans, leaving this ranch was something he'd never considered. Now he had no choice but to make different plans.

"How's his leg?" Chance asked from behind him.

"Looks better. He'll probably be out in the pasture by next week."

Chance joined him and looked out at the land, absently stroking Bodine's forehead. "We've had some good times here, haven't we?"

"Yep." Talon grinned as a scene played in his mind's theater. "You remember the time when we snuck out of the house around midnight and went camping over on the north side?"

"And that freak storm came up and scared our horses." Chance laughed. "They ran off and left us stranded. Man, it took us *hours* to walk all the way back in the dark. I don't remember ever being that cold."

"Yeah. Jake had the fireplace going for us, and Loretta made hot chocolate. Four o'clock in the morning. No telling how long they'd been waiting up."

"Jake didn't cut us any slack, though. Work starts at five a.m., no excuses."

"No excuses." A cloud of sorrow settled over Talon. He missed them. "They were good people."

Chance nodded and remained quiet for a few moments.

Talon looked over at him. "Thought about what you'd do if the ranch sold?"

"My mind's still working around it, but you know me–I'd rather ride a bull than brand one. I'd probably hit the circuit."

"I thought of that too. Not sure I like the idea." He huffed out a sigh. "What's going on in the bunkhouse?"

"The guys are getting ready for church. Not talking much." Chance gave Bodine a final pat. "You going with us?"

"Yeah." Talon gave the pasture one last look, then turned to the stable.

From her bedroom window, Patricia watched the trucks leave. Talon had said they would go to church this morning. Judging by all the sad faces, she felt they could've been going to a funeral. And she was to blame for the black mood that hovered over the ranch. Everyone hated her now.

Talon hated her.

Wrapping her arms around her waist, she remembered the

Give the Lady a Ride

firmness of his hands, the strength of his arms, the warmth of his smile as they'd walked together earlier. Not that it mattered now. He would revert to the impersonal politeness he'd exhibited when they first met. The sparkle she'd seen in his dark brown eyes wasn't likely to return.

She was such an idiot! Couldn't she have found a better way to answer Chance's question? Had she learned nothing during her years in political circles? Diplomacy was a daily part of her job. Delay tactics, white lies, spinning negatives into positives. She knew all the tricks and hadn't employed a single one of them. Where was her head? The fake smiles that came with her job were preferable to the stiff ones she'd find here after this morning.

Taking a breath, she shoved her fingers through her hair. No point dwelling on what was done and over. The proclamation of her plans finalized her decision to tend to business and go home. Any idea of staying here had been a daydream. A crazy one at that.

Uncle Jake's office needed her attention first. His insurance papers and anything else of importance were probably filed somewhere in there. She'd best start now, while Talon wasn't around to look over her shoulder.

She paused in the hall to listen by Marie's door. After their talk—or because of it—Marie had claimed to have a headache and had gone back to bed. The room was quiet, so Patricia slipped downstairs to the office, feeling like a spy in enemy camp.

The ledgers sat open on the desk where she and Talon had left them. She flipped them closed and pushed them aside for later. All the desk drawers were locked but the center one. She pulled it out, hoping to find the key to unlock the others. Pens, paper clips, and the usual items crowded the front, but the drawer was deep. She yanked it out farther, wincing at the wood-on-wood squeal, and slipped her hand in to feel around the back. Among the other odds and ends, she felt a key and drew it out. It was a tiny brass key, much too small for the desk drawers.

She glanced around, searching for whatever it might open. Jake's desk sat in the room's center, with a credenza behind it under the windows, and two brown leather chairs, dull and cracked with age, in front. A bookcase lined one side of the room with a beveled-glass display cabinet centered opposite it. She approached the cabinet and examined the lock embedded in the frame between twin glass panels. The key wouldn't fit, but the items inside drew her attention. A gentle tug on one door opened the cabinet, and she looked at the framed pictures inside. Candid shots of family, rodeos, and high school football games sat on the shelves. Standing tiptoe, she examined the pictures at the top. Talon and Chance grinned from each of them, teenagers in some, adults in others.

One small picture in the corner of the top shelf drew her eye. She stretched to pull it out. The image of her parents smiled back at her in faded color. Between them stood a five-year-old version of herself.

She reached to place the photo back on the shelf and saw another partially hidden behind one of Talon on a bull. In this picture, she was fourteen, sitting on the back of her rose-laden show horse, and grinning like the champion she'd been that day.

"What are you doing?" Marie stood in the doorway, rubbing her sleepy eyes.

"Look at this." Patricia held the frame up.

Give the Lady a Ride

"Yeah. Cute." She fluffed out her hair and yawned. "Where's the coffee?"

"Don't you get it?" Patricia pulled out the other picture of her and her parents. "Jake and Loretta kept up with me all those years, and I barely knew them."

"You were family."

"Not so you'd know it." She rubbed a finger across the photo glass. "Do you suppose that's why he wanted me to have the ranch? To keep it in the family?"

"What other reason would there be?" Marie pointed at the key Patricia had left on a low shelf. "What's that?"

She lifted the key for Marie to get a better look. "I don't know what it goes to."

"A key that small goes to something good." Marie rubbed her hands together. "Where do you want to start looking?"

"In here. If we don't find it, we'll move to the master bedroom." She grinned. "Nothing like a good treasure hunt to lighten the mood."

An hour later, Marie pulled an ornately carved Mexican letterbox from the credenza. "Looks like the key would fit this."

"Put it on the desk." Patricia pulled the key from the pocket she'd slipped it into and tried it. It fit, but the rusty lock wouldn't budge.

"We need some oil," Marie said.

"Kitchen." She grabbed the box and headed for the door.

Barking dogs and the crunch of tires on gravel drew Marie to the window. She pulled the shade aside and peeked out. "They're back."

Patricia took a quick look around the office. Drawers and

73

cabinet doors hung open, papers and pictures cluttered every flat surface. The room looked like it had been burglarized.

In a wave of panic, she put the box back on the desk, grabbed a stack of files and shoved it in a drawer. "Quick, we need to clean this place up."

"Why? Everything in here is yours."

"I know, I know. But it feels like we've been sneaking around." She thrust a pile of papers in the credenza. "Besides, it would be like rubbing salt in their wounds, and I feel bad enough as it is."

Marie dropped some snapshots back into the cabinet, then put her hands on her hips and scowled at Patricia. "If you want to stop feeling bad, figure out a way to keep the ranch."

Shoving a drawer shut with her hip, Patricia glared at her friend. "If you have any ideas, I'd love to hear them."

The front door opened and banged closed. Heavy footsteps crossed the linoleum floors, heading toward the kitchen.

Patricia grabbed the letterbox and hissed. "Let's get out of here."

Chapter Eight

"Maybe she didn't think of being an absentee owner." Chance jerked his dress boots off his feet and let them clunk to the bunkhouse floor. "Why don't you just ask her?"

Talon slipped out of his Sunday shirt and grabbed a green tee from the drawer. "Because it's best I don't talk to her right now. I've got to focus on my bull this afternoon, and I don't want anything else on my mind." He pulled the shirt over his head. "What makes you think she'd listen to me anyway?"

"You're kiddin', right? Didn't you see the way she was looking at you during breakfast?"

He'd seen . . . for what it was worth.

For a moment out in the back pasture, he and Pat had dropped their guard. Their conversation flowed easily, their laughter freely. He'd been mesmerized by the sun caressing her hair–hair the color of a Palomino colt.

He scowled. *Don't go getting poetic.*

Poetry had dried up in him eight years ago, and he didn't want to revive it now, especially over a woman who wanted to sell his home. The humor in her eyes, the music in her laughter, had lost their appeal this morning at the breakfast table.

"Doesn't matter how she looked at me now, does it?" he muttered and strode outside, slamming the door behind him. "C'mon, Oz."

He opened his pickup, and the dog jumped in. Talon followed.

"What about lunch?" Chance yelled from the bunkhouse.

Talon jammed the key in the ignition and drove away.

Somehow word had gotten out at church that the new owner of the Circle Bar planned to sell. Ranchers Talon knew and respected had turned into vultures, circling, swooping down to peck at him. *When will she sell? How much is she asking? Is the stock included? What about equipment?* Everyone seemed anxious for the Circle Bar's obituary to show up in the real estate pages.

Talon had walked the tightrope, neither denying nor confirming the sale, while testing the waters for possible employment.

He hated the responses. None of the ranchers were interested in taking on his whole crew. They'd employed all the hands they needed. And he could forget being a foreman. If he did find a job, he'd be just another cowboy learning to live and work with a different crew.

Only Ben Kilgore, owner of the Flying K, indicated he'd hire both Talon and Chance. Ben was a good man, a fair employer. He raised bucking bulls for rodeos and knew the benefits of hiring a couple of riders. If worse came to worst, Talon would take Ben's offer.

But he'd rather stay on the Circle Bar with his own crew and make his dreams for the ranch a reality.

Give the Lady a Ride

Oz caught the scent of livestock as Talon drove past the arena. His carefree barking did nothing for Talon's mood. In four hours, he would mount his last bull of the rodeo. He and Chance were tied one each so far in the competition. To win this weekend's event, he needed to draw a top bull and make the time. Probably wouldn't happen, but it would suit him fine if Chance took the purse.

"Settle down, Oz."

The dog delivered a final *woof!* and dropped his paws from the passenger window.

Talon rubbed his forehead. *Lord, I don't want to leave the Circle Bar. Please, tell me what to do.*

The gate to the cemetery was just ahead. Talon slowed and turned left.

"He's here!" Patricia pointed.

At chute gate three, Talon squirmed up a bull's brawny red back. Patricia crossed her fingers, holding them to her lips, and wished him a successful ride. His truck hadn't been in the parking lot when they arrived, and Patricia had worried he wouldn't make it. She and Marie had grabbed good seats on the second row, close to the chutes. They'd stood when cowgirls in fringed western shirts rode horseback around the arena with the flags. They'd sat through the bronc riding, the calf roping, and the barrel racing–all in anticipation of Talon's and Chance's rides.

"Chance said he wouldn't miss it." Marie barely got the words out before the gate flew open. The bull slung his flank to the right, and Talon flew off on the left. His ride was over.

"Not tonight, folks," the announcer said. "The best Talon

Carlson can hope for this time is a slot in second place."

Talon rose to his knee and bowed his head. Even without reason to think he would, Patricia hoped he'd search the crowd looking for her like Chance had for Marie the night before.

Instead, he watched his boots walk him out of the arena.

Disappointment dragged at her and vied with the anger boiling in her stomach. She was being silly. Her emotions ran way too high over a cowboy she'd known only two days. There was no excuse for it. She shouldn't be falling for a Texas bull rider when her father needed her in New York.

She *wasn't* falling for a Texas bull rider. People don't *fall* in two days!

Marie's squeal jerked Patricia from her thoughts.

". . . chute one, Chance Davis on the back of Red Stinger," the announcer said. "Now that Talon's out of the running for first place, Chance has a great shot at the buckle. He'll get a nice little check tonight if he makes the eight."

Chance had no problem with the bull's left spin, which seemed relatively easy on his sore shoulder, and he escaped unharmed after the eight-second horn sounded. He ran toward the stands, jumped up on the rails, and planted his boots on the second rung. "Come here, darlin'!"

Marie shot to the rail and wrapped him in her arms. He kissed her, earning hoots and applause from everyone around them, then grinned and dropped to the dirt. Before he jogged away, he tossed her his hat.

Marie propped the hat on her head and stepped over the first bench to return to her seat.

Patricia laughed. "You're acting like a woman in love."

"Yeah." Marie flashed perfect teeth. "What's your point?"

Give the Lady a Ride

Drawing her lips tight, Patricia studied her friend from the corner of her eye. Marie had lost her mind. There was no other explanation. She'd known Chance as long as Patricia had known Talon. No way she could be in love.

"It stinks back here." Patricia wrinkled her nose and swatted at flies as they passed the stock pens behind the arena.

"Well, walk faster," Marie ordered over her shoulder. "I want to see that buckle."

Beside his truck in the parking lot, Chance showed off his silver prize to the men surrounding him, with a huge grin stretched across his face. The guys slapped his back and shook his hand. Patricia couldn't hear their comments, only the resulting laughter. Marie marched through the cowboys crowded around him, took his hat off her head and positioned it on his, then wrapped him in another hug.

Patricia turned to look toward the other trucks in the lot. She couldn't bear to watch the lovebirds any longer. Talon passed nearby, and her unruly heart skipped a beat. He didn't even turn his head toward the crowd surrounding Chance and Marie. Once he reached his pickup, he tossed his gear in the back and climbed in. Gravel kicked up as he peeled out of the lot.

Patricia weaved past a couple of men to reach Chance's side. "Where's Talon going?"

Chance looked over his shoulder as Talon turned left onto the highway, then shrugged. "I reckon he's going back to the cemetery, ma'am. He goes there sometimes when he's got a lot on his mind."

The truck picked up speed on the asphalt, and Patricia felt a sudden rush of panic as it disappeared around a curve. She yanked her keys from her bag and jogged to her car, yelling over her shoulder for Marie to ride back with Chance.

Chasing Talon down like this was ridiculous. Patricia was being every bit as irrational as Marie, but she didn't care.

The speedometer on her Mercedes registered seventy-five. She pushed it to eighty.

What was she feeling? Not love, she knew that. Falling in love in two days was just as impossible as falling in love at first sight. It didn't happen. Attraction? Sure. But love?

Uh-uh.

Her tires squealed around a tight curve.

More than likely what she felt was guilt. She should've kept her mouth shut about selling the ranch. Had she not dumped that on him just hours before the rodeo, he would've made the time. If only she could explain, let him know why she needed to sell, maybe he'd understand.

If he didn't already hate her—but he probably did.

She saw the cemetery too late and left rubber on the road as she skidded to a stop. A driveway to her left provided a place to turn around, and she backtracked to the cemetery gates. Talon's truck sat inside the fence. She pulled in behind it and spotted him crouched under an ancient cedar beside a headstone midway across the grounds.

Whatever gave her the preposterous notion to follow him? She would obviously be intruding. What would she say?

She'd figure it out when she reached him.

He didn't look up as she approached. She stayed a short

distance back, still not knowing what to say. A pile of green weeds sat beside the plot, fresh dirt on their roots. Bright yellow black-eyed Susans and red Indian paintbrushes, tied into two clumsy bundles, rested on the graves. Talon had been busy this afternoon.

"He gave me my name, you know." His voice was so low she had to strain to hear.

She advanced a few steps, her hands clasped behind her back, and read the names on the headstone: Jake and Loretta McAllister.

"Tell me."

Talon brushed some cedar needles off the stone and rested his hand over Jake's name. "I didn't know a thing about ranching. My dad was a banker. Jake taught me everything I know about running a ranch. He said I was a fast learner, that I grasped what he was telling me like an eagle grips its prey. Eventually he started calling me Talon, and the name stuck."

"What's your real name?"

"Byron Earl Carlson." He snorted, twisting his head to look at her for the first time. "Do I look like a *Byron Earl* to you?"

She eyed his jeans and plaid cotton shirt, his black felt hat and dusty boots. If she didn't know him, she'd agree the name didn't fit. But she'd seen his confident stride and his quiet, commanding presence among the men . . . Yes, the name suited him.

American nobility in denim.

"I lived with Jake and Loretta until I turned eighteen and decided to join the men in the bunkhouse. That ranch has been my home since I was a kid. Can you understand how I feel about it?"

"Yes, I can. And I imagine it would hurt deeply to lose it." She closed the distance between them and sat cross-legged beside him on the grass. "Is that why you didn't ride well? Is it my fault you didn't make the time?"

Talon shook his head. "It was my own fault, ma'am. I just didn't have my head in the game."

She bristled when he called her *ma'am*, and longed to hear her name from his lips again. She wanted the intimacy back, the camaraderie they'd shared during their ride, the admiration he'd shown at breakfast. But what he said hadn't escaped her. "Then it *is* my fault. Your head wasn't in the game because you're worried about losing your home." When he didn't respond, she said, "I've thought about keeping it, about living here. But my job and my family are in New York. Moving here would be a gigantic step for me. And if I don't move, there would be no point in keeping the ranch. How could I run it from New York?"

"There is another option."

"What?"

"Let me run it. Just like I have for the past several years. I'd report to you like I did to Jake when he was alive, but long-distance. You'd get the profits and an account of the finances and stock."

She studied his dark eyes and saw the hope daring to appear, denying the ego of a man who would never beg, even to save his home. Here was a man of honest integrity and simple aspirations. When she compared him to the men she knew, with their expensive suits and ulterior motives . . . Well, there simply was no comparison.

Now she understood what Marie was feeling. Not love, but the potential for it.

Give the Lady a Ride

She shifted her gaze to a distant hill both shaded and highlighted by the late afternoon sun. A lone bird spread its wings in flight over a pasture nearby, covering the area swiftly until it landed in a tree and was no longer distinguishable in the shadows.

How quickly her time here had passed. It seemed to have flown by and disappeared as swiftly as the bird had. Tuesday would arrive before she knew it, and she'd have to leave, never knowing what might've happened between her and Talon.

She didn't want to go. She wanted to be like Marie and chase the potential. For the first time since her husband's death, her heart leapt at the prospect of falling in love again. Maybe this time, the man would be worthy of her devotion.

Talon's idea made perfect sense. But if she accepted his offer, she would still have no real reason to stay. The men could ship Jake's personal things to her in New York, and she and Marie could still catch their flight Tuesday. She needed more time.

A crazy idea developed in her mind and worked its way to her tongue. She grabbed a blade of grass to occupy her suddenly-nervous hands and cast him a sidelong glance. "Can you teach me to ride?"

"What?" His eyebrows shot up in such a comical look of surprise, she struggled to keep a serious expression.

"Teach me to ride bulls."

He shook his head, undoubtedly questioning her sanity.

"You don't think a woman can do it, do you?"

"No, I know women can ride. They have their own association." He tipped his hat back, his eyes glinted with challenge. "I just don't think *you* can do it."

Propping her fists on her thighs, she thrust out her chin. "Is that a dare?"

He laughed and flipped his hand up as if to dismiss the notion. "There are rodeo schools. I'll be glad to hook you up with one."

"No. I want you to teach me."

He dropped his head back on his shoulders and stared up at the lavender sunset. It was an idiotic idea, but he'd said women rode. Maybe it wasn't as crazy as she thought. She held her breath. Would he say yes? Would he realize why she asked?

"You're nuts, you know that?" He rose to his feet and offered her a hand. "It's getting dark. Let's get out of here."

She let him pull her up. "Is that a yes?"

"It's an 'I'll think about it.'"

Chapter Nine

Talon peered through the bunkhouse window, hesitant to go in. The Astros-Braves game blared from the TV, but no one paid much attention to it. Frank and Buster relaxed in fat recliners in front of the television, their socked feet kicked up and their noses buried in newspapers. Chance, dressed in his Sunday clothes, slid a comb through his hair in front of the mirror. If Talon walked fast and kept his head down, maybe he could get to his bunk without having to talk to anyone.

He almost made it.

"There you are," Chance said. "I've been wondering when you were coming back."

Talon swallowed a sigh and turned to face him. "Congrats on the buckle. That was a good ride."

"Thanks." Chance tossed his comb into a drawer and turned to him. "Did you talk to Pat?"

Frank and Buster swiveled in their seats to look at him. Hope mingled with the curiosity in their eyes.

Talon studied the floorboards. "I talked to her."

"Well?"

"Don't keep us waiting." Frank glowered at him from over his reading glasses. "What did she say?"

"She gonna keep the ranch?" Buster asked.

There wasn't a man in the room who didn't have a lot at stake. Frank had lived and worked on the ranch for forty years, and Buster for thirty. Neither had another place to call home. It rankled Talon to have no reassuring answers. "She didn't say."

Buster left his seat and strode closer. "Well, what *did* she say?"

"She wants to ride bulls."

The stunned silence was shattered with their deep chuckles.

Only Frank didn't laugh. "Wait a minute, boys, wait a minute. It takes time to learn to ride. Did you tell her that?"

"I didn't really discuss it with her."

"Give her some credit. I'm sure she realizes it'll take time." Frank rose from his recliner and limped across the room to join them. "She's on the fence. She hasn't decided for sure what she wants to do with the ranch. Could be she's buyin' time with this lame-brained idea."

"Does she want you to teach her?" Chance asked Talon.

"That's what she said."

Frank stroked his mustache and gave the group a sly grin. "Yep. Takes a long time to learn how to ride." His pale blue eyes shifted from Talon to Chance and back. "You boys better make good use of that time too."

"What do you mean?" Talon grew suspicious of the gleam in the old man's eyes.

"I ain't blind, son–those women are attractive. And I've seen how they look at you two." He swiveled a finger between them. "You need to make the most of that. As long as they're here, we've got a chance Ms. Talbert'll learn to like this place and won't want to sell. Once that happens, it won't matter. Whether she lives here or in New York, we'll stay on the ranch."

"Are you saying we should play up to the women to keep them here?" Talon scowled. "Isn't that a bit dishonest?"

"I've seen the way you and Ms. Talbert look at each other, boy. Trust me, it ain't dishonest. Just treat her the way you're a-wantin' to anyhow. Spend time with her. Show her around."

Talon opened his mouth to protest, then snapped it shut. He didn't know what he thought of Patricia Talbert yet, but there was no point arguing the fact. Although he found her attractive and enjoyed her company, he had no intention of getting serious. His belief that God wanted him single remained firm.

But, still, the idea of spending time with Pat wasn't exactly displeasing.

He caught a glimpse of a red-eared Chance staring at his boots with a goofy grin on his face. Apparently he had no complaints either.

"Hi, Daddy. Miss me?" Patricia rested against the worn oak headboard in her room and smiled into the phone.

"Pattie! How's my sweetheart?" The sound of her father's voice warmed her to her toes and burdened her with homesickness. She missed the smell of his aftershave, the gentle feel of his hand on her shoulder, the approval in his eyes for a job well done.

She swallowed back the wave of longing. "I'm fine. Is Marcy doing a good job for you?"

"Sure, sure. She's not you, but she's doing a fine job."

"Good. Can she do it a little while longer? I have more to do than I thought." It wasn't a total lie. She never thought she'd try bull riding–which did give her more to do.

"Do you need help with anything?"

"No," she said, a little too quickly. "There are quite a few papers to go through, several things to clear up. I should be able to get everything done before too long."

"That's fine then. Marcy's on top of things. Take all the time you need. What do you think of the place?"

"It's just beautiful. Rustic and rugged. Everything–every*one*– is so different." She twisted a strand of hair around her finger and looked out the window. In the driveway, Chance was helping Marie into his truck. Their laughter rang out in the evening air. Marie had said something about the movies as she darted past Patricia's room on her way out.

A twinge of envy fluttered in Patricia's chest. Marie slipped into relationships so easily.

"Sweetheart? You there?"

"Yeah, I'm here." She turned away from the window and sat cross-legged on the faded brown bedspread. "Dad, what happened between you and Uncle Jake?"

Silence stretched on the other end of the line. She could picture him rubbing the furrow in between his eyes. Maybe she shouldn't have asked. Maybe it was still too upsetting.

"Dad?"

"Let's just say legislation got in the way of sentimentality."

"What kind of legislation?" She ran ideas through her mind, landing on the one issue dearest to his heart. "Environmental?"

"Yes." She heard his resigned sigh and knew she would get the whole story. He drew a deep breath. "Several years ago, Jake

Give the Lady a Ride

heard of plans for a new highway expansion close to Fort Hood. He mortgaged the family ranch to buy some land surrounding the expansion hoping to sell it off at a higher price."

"Speculating."

"Right," he said. "Do you know what the Golden-Cheeked Warbler is?"

"A songbird?"

"Uh-huh. An endangered songbird. At least back then it was. I think their numbers are higher now. There was a heavy concentration of them around Fort Hood at the time, but their overall numbers were diminishing."

"Don't tell me. The expansion didn't go through?"

"No, it didn't." He was so quiet she could hear the squeak of leather in his favorite chair as he shifted his weight. "Jake couldn't sell the land and he couldn't develop it. He lost everything."

She bit her lip. "What about your half of the ranch?"

"I'd sold it to him years before. You know me. I wasn't interested in ranching."

"Poor Jake. That must've been awful for him. But I don't understand why he was angry with you. What did you have to do with it?"

His chair squeaked again. When he spoke, his voice was gruff. "I helped push through an amendment to the Endangered Species Act that included the bird for protection."

"Oh, no." Patricia rubbed her forehead. Her father had always stood up for what he believed in, but she had never known how much it cost him. She ached for him. "Jake landed on his feet, though, didn't he? How did he get this ranch?"

"Loretta's family. When he lost our place, they moved out to her dad's ranch and ran it for him. But her father didn't trust him after the fiasco in Fort Hood and willed the ranch to her as a *sole femme*. She must've left it to Jake when she died."

Two pictures emerged of the man who'd left her the ranch—a benevolent provider who took in teenage boys, and a failed entrepreneur who'd gambled away everything in a land deal and ended up living off his in-laws.

What had he really been like? Had he loved Loretta? Had she loved him? Patricia's eyes landed on the letterbox she had brought to her room earlier.

Were the answers in there?

After disconnecting with her father, she grabbed the box and carried it downstairs to the kitchen. Squelching the uneasy feeling that she was snooping, she oiled the lock with the WD-40 she'd found under the sink and raised the domed lid.

She lifted fifteen yellowed envelopes from the box. Beneath them rested a lock of Aunt Loretta's raven hair secured in a slender red bow and several Polaroid pictures. She eased out a snapshot of Jake and Loretta on horseback, holding hands and looking over their shoulders toward the camera. Another showed Loretta with a broad grin, holding up a string of fish. In another picture, a teenaged Talon stood in what looked like a river with Chance sitting on his shoulders, hands over Talon's eyes. She separated that one from the others to keep for herself.

Her stomach growled and she eyed the refrigerator, wondering if there was any blueberry cheesecake left over. There was.

Resting the snack and a soda on the table, she sat back down to pull the first letter out of its envelope. It was dated June15, 1965.

Give the Lady a Ride

My darling Jake,

Can you believe it's been five years? God blessed me so much when He gave me you. And, now, with this child I carry, I know He loves me. He must. No one in the world can be as happy as I am now.

If only there were words to express how very much I love you—I'd have them plowed out in the back pasture! I'd have them sky-written above the house! But the best I can do is just tell you: I love you.

Happy anniversary, Love.

They were in love. The pictures alone illustrated that, but the letter—what beautiful sentiments. Patricia grabbed another.

June 15, 1970
Jake, my love,

Who could've known the things we survived these past five years? God has truly blessed us with a strong bond. To lose two children! What parent can stand it? And yet, you were always there for me, and I for you. It may not be in God's plan to give us children, but I'll be forever grateful He gave me you.

Happy anniversary.

Patricia pushed her cheesecake aside and reread the letter

through the tears blurring her eyes. Oh, how she wished she could've known her aunt and uncle better. She hurt over the loss of their children. Their love for each other was astounding. It seemed strong, enduring, with an intimacy she had never seen in her parents' marriage, much less her own.

How could someone's faith in God remain that strong during the darkness of such pain? She believed in God too, when she thought about Him. Which wasn't often. He was a part of her life mentioned only in passing, called upon only in times of trial. Her parents were worldly. She was worldly. During her childhood, no one had broached spiritual issues, and as an adult, she rarely dwelt on them.

How different would her life have been under the influence of her aunt and uncle?

The first seven notes had been anniversary letters written five years apart. But after Loretta had been diagnosed with cancer, she wrote more often. She recorded her pride and her dreams for her "boys," Talon and Chance, and encouraged her husband to reconcile with his brother. She even gave instructions for her funeral. Never once did she express regret or anything less than total faith in the God she had trusted all her life. Tears stained many of these letters, and Patricia dampened them afresh with her own.

Thirty minutes later, she reached for the last letter and turned it over to find her own name in bold script. She stared. Jake had written her a letter and never mailed it? Her hands trembled as she opened it.

> Dear Pattie,
>
> First time I laid eyes on you, I figured there was nothing more beautiful on God's

green earth. You were quite a little lady, a good head on your shoulders and not a shy bone in your body.

We kept up with you over the years, Loretta and me. Your mother would tell us everything going on with you. We even saw you win one of your blue ribbons on TV. There were so many times Loretta wanted to have you out for the summer. I did too but didn't know how to ask. I'll always regret letting things between your father and me get so out of hand. Time moved on and I just never knew how to talk to him, how to say I was sorry for causing a ruckus over such a small thing. I forgave him years ago. I just hope he can forgive me.

I want you to have the Circle Bar. I want it to stay in the family like I wish the McAllister spread could have. But it's not just because you're family. It's because I want you to experience it.

The words blurred before her eyes. Her head spun, swirling together sadness and grief, anger and love. In the race around the track of her mind, anger won. Her father and Jake's stupid spat had deprived her of a relationship with two remarkable people, her aunt and uncle. They had loved her without even knowing her. And now, she knew she would've loved them. She ached with the loss.

Pat was crying. Talon tightened his grip on the doorknob and watched her through the window. Frank's plan dissolved, replaced by the uncertainty in his mind. Should he barge in, or slip away and respect her privacy?

With her sobs wrenching his gut, he shoved open the door and stepped inside.

Her shoulders tensed when she saw him. She sniffed and ran her fingers under her eyes. She may have wiped away the tears, but her red nose couldn't be so easily hidden.

He strode into the kitchen and stopped at her side. The old photos and papers scattered on the table piqued his curiosity. "Something wrong?"

"No, I'm okay."

She folded the page she was holding and pushed it into her shirt pocket where it peeked over the edge of the fabric, daring him to ask about it. Instead, he picked one off the table and read it.

"These are kind of private, aren't they?"

"Uncle Jake meant for me to read them. There was one addressed to me mixed in with the others."

"Well, maybe so, then." He reached for another and read of Mama Loretta's pride in him the first year he'd won a silver buckle. He swallowed hard against the lump in his throat. Lord, how he missed her, more than his own mother.

"They loved each other, didn't they?" Pat's voice was soft.

"Very much. Each other, God, the ranch, and all the men on it."

"Especially you and Chance."

"We loved them too." He pulled out a chair and dropped into it. "The men on this ranch owed them a lot. Jake was firm but

Give the Lady a Ride

fair, gave an honest day's pay for an honest day's work. He expected no more from the men than he was willing to do himself." The picture of Jake and Loretta on horseback made him smile. He picked it up for a better look, running his thumb lightly across the image. "Mama Loretta, we called her. She treated Chance and me like sons, the rest of the men like family. She kept us fed, tended our wounds, sat up with anyone who was sick–all the mom stuff. When Chance and I rode, the loudest voice in the stands was hers."

He saw Pat's untouched cheesecake and slid the plate to him. "Do you mind?" She shook her head, and he dug in. "Don't get me wrong," he said with his mouth full, then he swallowed. "She was tough. She rode a horse as well as any of the men. Could do any job on the ranch."

"Did she ever get mad?"

"Hoo! Did she *ever!*" He lowered his fork to the plate. "I remember her chasing me all the way around the house, swinging a broom at me like she was going to beat me half to death. Connected a few times too."

She laughed at the image; her red-rimmed eyes gleamed. The sound of her laughter warmed him like a fire on a cold morning. Like hot chocolate with marshmallows. What he wouldn't give to keep her laughing like that.

"What did you do to get her so mad?"

"She found out I'd been smoking up at the school. She chased me around–" he raised his hands in the air and swung an imaginary broom– "hollerin' *Don't you run from me, boy! You want to kill yourself, we'll just do it now!*"

Pat laughed until she hiccupped, and Talon laughed as much at her as his own story, surprised to see her shedding her rigid self-control.

When the hiccups subsided, she said, "Oh, I wish I'd known her."

"I wish you had too." Talon reached across the table and rested his hand on hers. His heart felt like it was going to swell up and bust right out of his chest. Only once before had he felt like that . . . He jerked his hand back and concentrated on the cheesecake. All Frank's scheming aside, he could really learn to like this woman. "Did you think anymore about being an absentee owner?"

"I did." She tilted her head; she had a look in her eyes, one that offered a challenge and dared him to accept. "Did you think about teaching me to ride?"

"I did."

Chapter Ten

"I thought we established that bull riding was crazy and bull *riders* are insane!"

Patricia could hear the incredulity in Marie's voice from inside the dressing room of a local western-wear store. She slid into a pair of stone-washed jeans and peeked over the cubicle's saloon doors. "It was the only reason I could think of to stay on for a while."

"We saw tons of paperwork in the office. That alone would've kept you here for a few weeks."

"But it wouldn't have kept me near Talon."

"And the truth comes out." At the dressing rooms' entrance, Marie crossed her arms and leaned against the doorframe. "What did your dad say about you riding?"

"Are you kidding? I didn't tell him!"

"That's right, you didn't tell him. He'd be here before noon and whip your pretty little bubble butt all the way back to Manhattan. Wouldn't matter to him that you're over thirty."

Patricia laughed. Marie knew her father well.

"What are you going to do about the ranch?"

Linda W. Yezak

"I wish I knew." Patricia stepped out of the dressing room and examined the jeans in a three-way mirror. *Bubble butt* was right. "How was your date with Chance?"

Marie's voice turned dreamy. "They don't make them like that in New York."

"Yeah, he's a nice guy." Patricia eyed her through the mirror. "But really, I can't believe you're attracted to him. He's a kid."

"He's a year older than we are."

"*Really?* He looks twenty."

"Must be all this clean air." Marie fingered the fringe on a teal and white rodeo shirt hanging next to the dressing rooms' entrance. She lifted it off the rack and held it up to herself in front of the mirror. "You'd think after riding bulls and being all macho, he'd be a testosterone-laden jerk, but he's sweet. And funny." She rolled her head toward Patricia. "And more intelligent than you give him credit for. He went to college, you know."

"He did?"

"Both of them did. Chance graduated a year after Talon with an Ag-Eco degree."

"Let me guess. Agricultural Economics?"

"Give the girl a gold star." Marie hung the shirt up and reached for a red one. "So when do the lessons begin?"

"Later this afternoon." Patricia looked her over. She wore designer labels from head to foot. "Are you planning to watch?"

Marie shrugged a shoulder. "Sure, why not?"

"Then you'd better start shopping. Prada and cow manure won't mix."

"I can't believe *you* and cow manure would mix." Marie read the brand name posters hanging throughout the store and wrinkled her nose. "Guess it'd be a waste of time to ask for Gloria Vanderbilt."

On the Circle Bar, the old cattle chute on the south side of the working pens was similar to a rodeo chute. The tailgate allowed the animal in, and the head gate kept it there. Then there was the side gate. From here, the animal–whether a bronc or a bull–could explode into the largest working pen and put on a show. This gate, the least used on the chute, refused to open no matter how hard Talon tugged. "You got a steel brush in that box?"

Chance rummaged through his tools and brought one out. "Can't believe how rusty the hinges are. Guess it's been awhile."

"Since the last bull Jake put me on when he was teaching me to ride." Talon dropped to one knee beside the top hinge and scrubbed it with the brush. "Did I tell you Ben Kilgore would take us on if we have to leave the ranch?"

"Working on a rodeo ranch would be a good job. More complex than just raising cows."

"Yeah. We'll be able to put our genetics classes to good use." Red dust coated Talon's hands and peppered the air, tickling his nose. He twitched and ran the back of his hand under his nose, giving himself a rusty mustache, then scoured the next hinge.

Chance stooped next to him with a scraggly paintbrush and dusted the first hinge clean. He reached back for the oil gun. "Can you believe you're fixing to teach some five-foot-nothin' Yankee woman how to ride a bull?"

Talon snorted. "Nope."

"You going to start her out on Bart?"

"No, I'm going to follow Frank's advice and take it slow. Real slow. Don't want to put her on a bull right now. It'd be our luck she'd consider herself a pro the first time she stayed on longer than three seconds, then hightail it back home," he eyed Chance from beneath his hat brim, "and take Marie with her."

Chance's face flushed redder than the rust. He squirted oil on Talon's hand, turning the dust into a greasy red sludge.

Talon laughed and rubbed the mess off on Chance's jeans. "Admit it, you want more time with her. You're not in a hurry for them to leave."

"Don't you want more time with Pat?" Chance rocked back on his heels. "You know, she acted kind of weird after the rodeo last night."

"Weird? What do you mean?"

"She saw you leave and took out after you like she had a wolf on her tail. I don't think she even looked both ways before squealing onto the blacktop." He chuckled. "Her speed could've qualified for NASCAR."

Talon knew she must've flown down the highway because he'd barely reached the headstone before he heard her tires screech and saw her turn around. The moment she pulled into the cemetery grounds, he had prayed for guidance. Only God's direction could have allowed him to be civil after the day he'd had. But the humble way in which she'd approached him melted his anger, and he'd found himself willing to talk, to tell her what was on his mind.

"She seems to be a good woman." Talon's knee creaked when he stood. "But that doesn't change the fact she's our boss, at least for now."

Give the Lady a Ride

He dropped the steel brush into the toolbox while Chance oiled the last hinge, then he tested the gate. It swung open with a soft, mousy squeal and closed again without protest.

"Yeah, she's our boss." Chance grinned up at him. "But that doesn't change the other fact–you're attracted to her."

"Sure I am. Who wouldn't be?" But nothing would ever come of it.

"You sure you want to do this?" Talon asked Patricia as he climbed the three concrete steps to join her and Buster on the platform behind the chute. Below them just outside the pen, Chance and Frank manned the side gate.

She nodded and shoved her new tan Stetson tighter on her head. Before bringing her out to the chute, Talon had given her a thirty-minute seminar on the basics. He'd said he wanted to start her out with the bull rope on a horse, so she could get used to the rope before she graduated to the tame breeder bulls. From the breeders, she'd move to the young steers which were wilder, but nothing like rodeo bulls.

Patricia stretched each leg on a rail to limber up. Her brown Justin boots fit snug on her feet, and her jeans had a little give to them. All in all, the clothes were comfortable enough. The leather glove on her right hand was just a hair too big. Talon had taped it over her wrist so it would stay on during the ride.

"Bring Tandy in," he ordered.

Frank pulled the tailgate on the chute's right side. Tandy ambled in with a lunge rope draped across his withers and a nylon bull rope wrapped around his chest. Patricia's nerves twitched as she stared at the braided handle looped over the leather strap on the bull rope. Talon had said when Chance pulled that rope, it would tighten around both Tandy and her hand–her only grip during the entire time she was on Tandy's back.

Well, she could also grip with her legs. She had strong legs. And this was just *Tandy*. It wasn't like she was getting strapped onto a bull. This was just for practice. She shouldn't have any trouble with the ride . . . Right?

Talon took Patricia's elbow and searched her eyes. "Okay. You know what to do. You ready?"

Butterflies flitted in her stomach. She rolled her tight shoulders and flexed her hands. If she felt like this before riding a horse–something she'd done for years–how would she feel facing a bull?

But she'd asked for it. "I think so."

"Okay, then." He turned her toward the chute rail and gave her a pat on the back. "Get 'er done."

Hanging onto the rail, she climbed over the back of the chute, then reached for the opposite rail and slid her legs around Tandy's dappled gray sides.

"Now, slip your hand into the rope–no, palm up."

She flipped her hand over so the back rested on the leather strap just behind Tandy's withers, and gripped the braided handle.

"There ya go." He leaned over the back of the chute, keeping a hand on her shoulder. "When you're ready, give Chance a nod so he can tighten the rope. He'll hand you the slack."

She nodded, and Chance, standing on the third rail of the side gate, pulled up on the rope.

Patricia winced and wiggled her fingers in the glove.

"Too tight?" Chance eased the tension a bit. "You don't want it too loose or it'll slide, and you may as well be hanging onto air."

He handed her the tail of the rope, and she wrapped it around her hand one more time, making sure it was secure, just as Talon had taught her.

"Is it snug?" he asked.

She nodded. "It's good."

"Then you're ready. Now, work your way forward. I don't want you sitting on your hand, but you need to be right close."

Patricia grabbed hold of the fence with her free hand and scooted her feet along the lower rails toward Tandy's withers until her thigh bumped her wrist. Then she sat firmly on the horse's back and wrapped her short legs around his sides the best she could.

"You settled in?" Talon tested the rope with a slight tug, then patted her gloved hand.

She took a deep breath and huffed it out. "I'm ready."

Chance whipped open the gate, and Buster gave the horse a nudge with his foot. Tandy lumbered out of the chute with a bored been-there-done-that gait, and gave Patricia a slow tour of the pen.

"Keep your free hand up," Talon called from the platform. "Hand up, chin down."

Hand up, chin down. Toes out, heels in. Patricia's mind reeled with all of Talon's instructions.

With a limping gait, Frank jogged toward them, grabbed the lunge line from Tandy's shoulders and led the horse to the center of the ring. He clicked his tongue, urging Tandy to trot in a circle around him.

From the chute platform Talon called, "Do you feel the

rhythm?"

She felt it. Bouncing on Tandy's back without the steadying effect of stirrups, she definitely felt it.

"Yee-haw!" Marie sat on the top fence rail next to the chute and waved the white Stetson she'd bought earlier; the red fringe of her rodeo shirt swayed with the movement. "Ride him, cowgirl!"

Patricia felt her vertebrae jar each time she pounded on Tandy's bare back. It took all her willpower not to hold on with both hands, not to kick the horse into a gentler, more comfortable lope.

Cowgirl? She didn't think so.

"Okay, now, dismount," Talon yelled.

"So soon?"

"Now!"

She opened her hand and slipped her leg over the horse while twisting to the left–all at once, just as he had taught her. She dropped to the ground in a motion so swift she couldn't get her footing and fell laughing to her knees.

"Get up! Get up!"

The urgency in Talon's voice spurred her to scramble toward the chute and jump to the rails.

"Right there's the most dangerous time of the ride." He frowned. "You've got to get up and clear the arena. You could get hurt. Seriously hurt. And even if you *are* hurt, you've still got to get up or you could get killed."

During his thirty-minute lecture, he'd told her that more than once. Next time, she'd get it right.

"Okay," he said. "Let's do it again."

After Patricia's fourth time around on Tandy, Marie became

bored and hollered that she was going in for a shower. After the sixth time, Patricia was ready to climb down Talon's throat and yank out his vocal chords.

Though every round had been the same, he'd wanted her to go again. It was dark out now. Bugs flew around the mercury lights, buzzed near her ears, and snagged in her hair. Her body hurt. She was sweaty and filthy, and stunk of horsehide and dirt. As she limped back to the chute–again–she longed for a hot bubble bath in the claw-foot tub upstairs in the ranch house.

"Cowboy up!" Chance yelled to her. "You can go another round."

She snarled at him.

Brushing off her stained britches, she planted her feet in front of the gate and squinted up at Talon's backlit silhouette. "When can I ride a real bull?"

Talon leaned on the rail. "When I think you're ready."

She thrust out a hip to prop her gloved fist on and waved her free hand in the air. "I don't understand. Why can't we just get one of the calves from the pasture and let me ride him?"

Frank grinned at his boots. Buster choked on a chuckle.

"Sure, Talon." Chance draped an arm around her, his lips quirked up. "Why don't we just let her ride one of the yearlings?"

Talon disappeared from behind the chute and reappeared beside the pen gate. "You must be tired. Let's call it a day."

She hobbled toward him. "You didn't answer me."

"It's not a good idea to put you on a calf yet."

"Why not?"

The men behind her snickered again, and she whipped around to face them. "What's so funny?"

"Ben Kilgore's bucking the babies tomorrow on the Flying K," Talon said. "If you want to know why it's too early to put you on a calf, you can find out then."

Chapter Eleven

A t the Flying K Ranch the following afternoon, Patricia grabbed a seat on a square hay bale and propped her boots on the bottom rung of a maroon pipe fence. The arena on the other side of the fence was larger than the pen she'd ridden Tandy in last night, and sandy rather than packed with dirt. The steamy afternoon air was redolent with hay and livestock and spiced by angry bellows from the pens beyond the arena.

This was nothing like she'd expected. No cowboys rode horseback, no dogs barked and nipped at the animals. Only Talon and a couple of men sitting on the rails at the far side of the arena wore cowboy hats. The others were in caps. No one wore the highly-starched shirts she'd seen at the rodeo, just tees. She laughed when she read the back of one of them: *Scars are just tattoos with better stories.*

"What's the difference between a rodeo ranch and the Circle Bar?" she asked.

Talon, standing with his arms crossed on the fence, looked over his shoulder at them. "We raise beef cattle. We want our

Linda W. Yezak

bullocks eating and bulking up, not fighting. So we take the urge to fight away from them. Ben raises his bulls for riding, so he wants them athletic. He wants the fire in their bellies."

Even with her sunglasses, Marie had to cup a hand over her eyes to look at him. "How does he know which bulls will make good buckers?"

"Genetics play a big part in it, but what he's doing today will give him a good idea." Talon climbed the rails and gazed to the pens beyond the chute. "Looks like the last of the three-year-olds is in the chute."

A black, hump-shouldered bull reared up against the plywood panel at the front of the chute and tossed his horns. Patricia gawked at the animal's bulk. He seemed almost as big as the bulls Talon had ridden. "He's huge."

Talon dropped from the fence rails. "He's a thousand, maybe up to twelve hundred pounds."

The bull pawed at the panel as if he could scramble over it. The board itself must've been five feet high, and the animal towered over it. One of the men at the chute rapped its nose, and the bull sank to all fours.

"That's Cody with the stick, his brother Colton on the right, and Jim on the left." Chance pointed at each one. "Mark and Tom are at the gate."

None of the tanned young men looked much older than twenty.

Tom pulled a long, slender hook off a rail and reached below the belly of the bull, pulling up the rope end Cody had dropped. Cody held one end, Tom the other. Both leaned over the back of the bull.

Marie nudged Chance. "What are they doing?"

108

Give the Lady a Ride

"Tying on the flank strap. That's what makes a bull kick and extend his back legs like he does. It has to be tight enough to stay on, but loose enough that he thinks he can kick it off. It'll come off easily–but not as easy as he thinks."

Patricia watched the bull kick the back panel as the men tried again to tie the strap on him. "I've heard that–"

Talon held up a hand. "Everyone's heard that. But it's not true. No part of the bull's anatomy is tied the way you're thinking. And no cattle prods are used to urge bucking. The bull bucks because he wants the ropes off–the ropes and that box they're strapping on him now. See that?" He pointed to a small, metal cube, maybe twelve by eight inches, mounted on leather straps. A slender rope with a steel pin at the end dangled from one of the straps. "It's a twenty-eight pounder called a bucking dummy. They're strapping it behind his shoulders now. Ben over there has the remote." He jerked a thumb toward a man in his fifties with sandy hair. "He can poke a button and the box falls off immediately, taking the flank strap with it."

When Cody nodded, Mark pulled the chute gate. The bull stormed out and charged toward the spectators. He slammed into the fence a foot away from Patricia. Face-to-face with the animal, she jerked her legs back from the rail and slapped a hand over her pounding heart. The bull's brown eyes rimmed white with terror as he registered her presence. Digging his hind hooves in, he turned and showered her with sand in his frantic retreat.

"Oh, wow." She brushed off her shirt and jeans and darted a glance at a wide-eyed Marie doing the same. "Oh, wow!"

"You sure you want to ride that thing?" Marie flicked a finger toward the panting calf.

She laughed. "Well, maybe not *that* one."

"You think smaller ones will be easier?" Talon flashed that annoying grin again, the same one all the men had worn last night when they'd smiled at some private joke at her expense. Maybe her reaction to whatever was going to happen would put an end to their amusement. For now, she settled for a one-shouldered shrug.

But a moment later, she gaped while a calf not much bigger than those cute little babies she'd seen a few days ago rammed his head into the front of the chute. His back hoof flew up, catching Colton in the soft spot of his shoulder.

"Aw, *man!*" Colton grabbed his injury and swung away from the chute, his exclamations muffled with the activity below him.

"Push it! Push it!" Cody yanked the cord used to unlock and open the chute gate, and Mark shoved the gate to the far back corner, forming a triangle around the calf to reduce the amount of space he had to buck in. The calf kicked again and entangled his back legs in the gate. Jim grabbed the animal's tail, lifted him off the rails, and settled him back in the chute.

"That one's about four hundred pounds." Talon's voice was tinged with the humor of another teasing jab, but Patricia couldn't tear her eyes from the action long enough to glare at him.

The calf's white head was barely visible over the wood panel at the bottom of the side gate. The most she'd seen of him were horns and hooves.

So much power in that little package.

The calf exploded from the chute with all the fury of his larger cousins. His hind legs slashed the air and stabbed it with a kick. He twisted and bucked, spraying dirt and bawling. On the second toss of his rump, the metal dummy and flank strap fell away.

Give the Lady a Ride

With his black nose flaring and his ears twitching, the calf crouched on his front legs and cast terrified eyes around him. Then he flicked his tail and darted to the far side of the arena, away from all things human.

Patricia blew out a breath and glanced at Talon to find him watching her with that amused grin on his lips.

"What do you think now?"

She pushed her hair out of her eyes. "I think I'm going to stick to your game plan."

Ben's wife, Sadie, knew how to treat both ranch hands and visitors. All afternoon, she'd been grilling hamburgers and hotdogs, simmering a pot of beans, making potato and macaroni salads, and baking peach cobblers and pecan pies. Under a white garden canopy, a long table draped in a red checked cloth supported the weight of the steaming dishes and platters loaded with the meat and trimmings. An ice chest at the end of the buffet line held any kind of soda a person could want. In a yard landscaped with rock gardens and burnt orange lantanas, picnic tables crowded with hungry cowboys huddled under shade trees.

Since Talon had spent so much time discussing ranching and livestock with Ben out by the arena, he was the last in line. He set himself up with a hamburger and glanced over his shoulder while he waited for the line to move. Chance had shepherded the women to a shaded table far from the ranch hands and was now cramming half a hotdog into his mouth. The man's table manners weren't likely to impress his lady love.

"Jealous?"

"What?" Talon turned. Sadie had a scoop of beans for him, and he held his plate so she could ladle them on.

"I asked if you were jealous." From a face lightly scarred with healed skin cancers and a half-century's worth of wrinkles, shone a pair of blue eyes bright with mischief. "Chance is getting all the attention while you're wasting time talkin' bulls with Ben."

"He'd probably get all the attention anyway."

"Them the women from up north? The ones who own Jake's ranch?"

"The short one is. The tall one just tagged along."

Sadie plopped a spoonful of potato salad on his plate and tilted her head. "I've seen the way that little one looks at you. Saw her at the rodeo, holding her breath while you rode. Or *tried* to ride."

Talon rubbed at the heat climbing the back of his neck. "You saw that, did ya?"

"Never miss a local rodeo." She moved along her side of the table. "Pie or cobbler?"

"Can I have both?"

"Sure." On an extra plastic plate, she scooped him a serving of each. "You know you can have both of the others too."

"Other what? What do you mean?"

"You can have the ranch and the lady too. If you play your cards right."

"Now, Ms. Sadie, I've been out of the game for years."

"I know." She tightened her lips. "It's time for you to get back in. You deserve to be happy, Talon."

He twisted in time to catch Pat rubbing a drop of mayo off her chin with a paper napkin. She laughed, and the sound floated to him like wind chimes in the breeze.

Give the Lady a Ride

Sadie had slipped beside him and rested a hand on his shoulder. "It's time, honey. Time for you to go on and live a little."

From across the lawn, Pat locked eyes with him, and her lips curled into a sweet smile. Talon's heart turned to mush. "Yes ma'am, Ms. Sadie. Maybe you're right."

Chapter Twelve

Talon had never seen anything so beautiful, and he wasn't thinking of the hawk swooping down from a clear morning sky to catch its prey. Pat turned in her saddle and watched the bird. Her hair blew in the breeze like soft winter wheat. Her face, scrubbed clean of all makeup, glowed with an energy not bottled by Cover Girl. When she focused on him, her eyes were bright and lively. He wanted to gather her in his arms and waltz across the meadow, lost in those dancing green eyes.

"Did you see that?" Her voice was breathless. "That rabbit must've weighed as much as he did."

He shifted his eyes to the bird, watched it fly low with a young, squealing jackrabbit in its claws. "Strong bird."

"Does he have a nest somewhere?" She hesitated and gave him a quizzical look. "Or is it an aerie? Is the bird female? Does she have little ones?"

He couldn't stop the chuckle escaping his lips. "I take it you don't have hawks in New York."

"Of course we do. Just not in Manhattan."

She nudged Tandy's ribs and resumed the ride at an easy pace. With a click of his tongue, Talon urged Sable to pull alongside her. The men usually rode the four-wheelers to check the fence line, but this morning he'd thought it would be more fun on horseback with her. He was right. He'd been too busy watching her to even notice the fence.

She sat the horse like she was born on it, despite the fact she was probably still sore from her first bull riding lesson. But she hadn't complained. In fact, she didn't seem to talk much at all. Other than the few questions she'd asked about things she saw along the ride, she seemed content to enjoy the peace.

Not that he minded the sound of her voice, and he'd get to listen to it for as long as she owned the Circle Bar. For the sake of everyone on the ranch, he needed to know how long that would be. "So, did you make it to the realtor's Monday?"

"We went shopping instead." She swept a hand from her plaid sleeveless top to her denim clad thighs. "Didn't you notice?"

Oh, yeah, he'd noticed while he was teaching her to ride Monday evening. And again Tuesday at the Flying K, where she'd worn her sensible brown boots, a striped top, and Wranglers like the ones hugging her hips today. While he admired her game-for-anything spirit, he also admired the package that spirit came wrapped in. She did good things to western wear.

She laughed. "So you *did* notice."

His neck grew warm as he snapped his gaze back to her eyes. "Hard not to."

She tilted her head and sent him a glance from the corner of her eye. "Good. I didn't waste my money then."

"Oh, no ma'am, you sure didn't." Talon shifted his focus to the fence. No way could he look at her and dig for information at the same time. He needed to keep his mind on business. "Boys are kind of wondering what's in their future. Have you made a decision?"

She sighed, and for several long minutes afterward, the only sound was the horses snorting.

"Marie and I were supposed to be back in New York Tuesday instead of watching the calves buck. Did you know that?"

He shook his head. Hope reared its head, but her tone chased it away.

"Dad's up for his re-election this year. He's in the middle of his campaign, and I should be home managing fund raisers." Her lips twisted into a smile. "But here I am, learning to ride bulls."

"So, what does that mean? Are you keeping the ranch?"

"I wish I knew what it meant." She flipped a hand in the air. "Yes, I'm considering keeping it. And I'm considering *not* keeping it. And I'm considering being an absentee owner." Shy embarrassment tinged her smile. "You probably won't believe me, but I'm usually far more decisive than this."

"Oh, I believe you. I'm sure the work you do demands snap decisions, and I'm sure you're capable of making them or you wouldn't still have your job." He reached out and rubbed her shoulder until the horses drifted apart. "A life-changing decision like this one shouldn't be made in a snap. I'm glad you gave yourself more time. Have you prayed about it?"

"Prayed?"

"Sure. A question this hefty needs God's guidance." Her brows dipped between her eyes, and he mentally smacked his head. "Sorry. Didn't mean to preach. I forget not everyone is a Christian."

"Oh, no–I'm a Christian. Just . . . not a good one. I'm afraid

He hasn't heard my voice in quite a while."

"Maybe it's time He did. Take your troubles to Him and have faith that He'll help you out in time." *And Lord, no need to rush.*

"So, how did your ride go this morning?" Marie's fork hovered over a slice of the diner's lemon meringue.

"Good, until he asked me what I'm going to do about the ranch."

"What *are* you going to do?"

"That's just it—I don't know." Patricia picked at her plate, clinking the fork against the heavy stoneware. She detested indecision, but simply could not make up her mind. Should she stay, gamble that something would develop between her and Talon? Or should she do the sensible thing and get back to work? But she was learning to love it here. The sun on the hills, the gentle nights. The soft thrum of a quieter pace.

Talon was right. This shouldn't be a snap decision. She needed more time to explore what this life had to offer. "I'd like to stay a little while longer. I think Marcy can cover for me. Do you need to get back to your shop?"

"What are they going to do? Fire me?" Marie laughed. "Extending my vacation is a benefit of being the owner." She shoved a bite of the pie in her mouth and pointed at Patricia with the fork. "You belong here, you know. You're freer here. More daring. More alive than I've seen you in years. And I've never heard anything more outlandish come out of your mouth than wanting to ride bulls. Manhattan never brought that sense of adventure out in you."

Give the Lady a Ride

"I do love it here, but I can't say I *belong* here. What about my job? What about New York? I love New York!"

"No you don't." Marie dabbed a napkin to her lips. "You hate your life there. You've told me so yourself. Recently."

The words slapped like an accusation, and an odd sense of loyalty flooded her. "It's my life. It's familiar."

"It's a bore."

"How can you say that? The parties, the dances, the fund raisers—I'm *somebody* in Manhattan."

"You're the same thing you are here. A senator's daughter. You need to do something for yourself." Marie took a deep breath. "Look, Pattie, you light up every time you see a horse, and I know that ride at break-neck speed Sunday morning made your blood pump." She held up her hand to halt Patricia's interruption. "Yes, we have horses in New York, but it's time you broke away—spread your wings. You've lived a safe life for way too long. Our apartment is right down the street from your parents. You see your dad almost every day when he's in New York, and when he's not, you make several trips to DC to meet with him. Your life is held in one big safety net. Girl, you've gotta cut a hole in it and fall through!"

"I don't know. Maybe you're right." But she was so sick of talking about it. She grabbed her fork and nipped the tip off the wedge of her chocolate pie. "If I moved here, you'd miss me. Don't deny it. You know you would."

"Of course I would." Marie gave her a wicked smile. "But only if you went back to New York."

"Wait. I don't understand." She propped her elbows on the table and rested her chin on her fists. "Talk."

"Chance wants me to stay."

Patricia opened her mouth to protest, but Marie waved her off.

"Don't. Just hear me out." She pushed the rest of her pie aside and leaned closer. "Pattie, I think this is it. Capital *I*, capital *T*. I know it's just been a short time. I know it doesn't make sense. And you know me–I can't even count how many boyfriends I've had." Her face softened. "But this is different. This is so . . . wonderful. He's a Christian, and he's really making me want to be one too. He's just special. I can see myself settling down with him."

"Are you telling me you're getting married?" Patricia slowly shook her head. She'd never seen Marie like this. "You barely know him."

"No, no. I'm not saying that." A smile tugged at her lips. "At least not yet."

"What about your shop?"

"I'll open one here."

Tapping her plate with the fork, Patricia stared at her until she shifted in her seat.

"I know, I know. Liz Claiborne may be a bit out of place out here. But I can sell the thorns off a cactus. I'll come up with something."

Marie was so confident. Why couldn't Patricia be daring like that? Just drop everything and start a new life. "Talon said I should pray before I decide what to do. Did you pray?"

Marie's cheeks flushed as she nodded. "Chance and I prayed together. His faith is one of the special things about him."

Patricia nodded. Talon's faith was special too. Had he learned it from Loretta? Kent had shattered Patricia's faith in herself; if she stayed at the ranch, would she regain her faith in God?

Give the Lady a Ride

Frank and Chance were deep in the hay baler, wrangling a belt into place, when Talon found them.

Frank flashed him a glance. "How'd the ride go?"

"She hasn't made a decision, if that's what you're asking." Talon watched them work.

"That's what I'm askin'. Keep working on her." Frank elbowed Chance. "Chance and Ms. Marie are getting pretty serious."

Chance's grin stretched from one red ear to the other. "She's something."

"They're both something."

The belt slipped into place. Frank gave a satisfied smile and grabbed a rag to wipe his hands. His mustache twitched as he regarded Talon. "I saw you writing in your journal last night."

Talon shifted uncomfortably. He'd thought everyone was asleep when he went on his midnight writing spree. Spending so much time with Pat had awakened the poet in him, and he hadn't been able to shove down the words.

"C'mon, 'fess up." Chance jabbed his shoulder. "You're love-bit."

Talon looked out toward the pasture. "The only thing I'll 'fess up to is that I find her attractive. I don't believe in love at first sight."

"I didn't either."

"You saying you're in love?" Chance's red face told him everything he needed to know. Talon blew out his breath. "It hasn't even been a week, Chance. Are you sure?"

"Sure enough to know that if it's not love, it soon will be." He rested a hip on the baler. "I've asked her to stay in Texas."

Talon shook his head. "I hope you know what you're doing."

"Chance wouldn't ask her lightly," Frank said. "What did she say?"

"She's thinking about it." Chance slapped Talon's back. "Don't worry about me. Annie taught me a lot about what love *isn't*."

He circled the baler, gathered the tools they'd used to repair the belt, and headed to the toolbox. Talon watched him, thinking about his two-year relationship with Annie. She'd led him on, letting him spend what money he had on her while stringing along some other poor sap in Stephenville. Chance had moped around the bunkhouse like a lost puppy for months after he'd found out.

Frank cleared his throat. "It's fine that you took Ms. Talbert out on the spread today, and it's fine you're teachin' her how to ride bulls. But Chance's got the right idea. He and Ms. Marie go on dates. You 'member what those are, don't ya?"

"I thought the plan was to get her liking *the ranch* so she wouldn't sell it."

"Nothin' in the rule book says ya can't get her to likin' you too."

Frank, Chance, even Sadie at the Flying K had hinted for Talon to get back into the dating game. *Out of the mouths of two witnesses shall a thing be established.*

For the first time in eight years, obedience to God's will seemed a burden. Was it possible God hadn't meant him to be single? Maybe he was just supposed to wait. Was Pat the one he'd been waiting for?

He hoped so. He couldn't take another loss.

Chapter Thirteen

Patricia's mouth dropped as a brawny Angus bull the size of the Flying K's three-year-olds entered the chute.

"That's Black Bart," Talon said. "He's one of our breeding bulls. He'll give you a fair ride, but he's tame as a kitten. He'll buck and kick some, but nothing you can't handle."

She eyed the sheer bulk of the animal. "I hope you're right."

Bart stood patiently while Buster and Frank tied on the bull rope. No lunge rope this time, as there had been on Tandy. Patricia would be riding the bull without Frank prompting him to trot.

She rolled her shoulders, bent to touch her toes, and swiveled her hips to stretch her legs. Maybe she *was* ready. At the baby bucking, she'd watched the calves carefully. Most of them had run out, kicked the air, and twisted a bit to the right. Bart would probably do the same.

Feeling a little more confident, she climbed on, strapped in, and gave the nod as if she'd been doing this for years.

"You can do it, girl," Marie called from the pen rail.

Bart jumped from the chute and twisted left before his hooves landed. Patricia hit the ground hard on her tailbone while he lumbered to some grass in the corner of the pen.

"Get up. Let's go again." Talon said.

Chance herded Bart back to the chute. Patricia mounted, strapped, and nodded. Bart ran out, twisted left, kicked dirt into the air. She landed on her back this time, got up, and scrambled to the chute.

"I don't get it." Brushing herself off, she looked up at Talon behind the chute. "All the bulls yesterday twisted right."

"Bart favors his left side, but you can't anticipate what a bull will do. You'll land in the dirt every time."

"This time," Marie yelled. "I have faith in you, kiddo!"

The third time Bart twisted right. Patricia dropped with a thud.

"That settles it." Talon came down from the platform. "Chance, get that two-by-four from the barn and bring it out here."

As Chance jogged toward the barn, Talon entered the pen and waved Patricia over to him. He rested his hands on her shoulders.

"You're trying to guess what he's going to do. You can't do that. You have to *feel* it. Blank your mind out and just feel it."

When Chance returned with an eight-foot beam balanced on his shoulder, Talon took it and placed it on the rough ground. Buster and Frank moved closer, and Marie jumped down from the fence to stand by Chance.

"I want you to walk across this board, from one end to the other." Talon put his arm around Patricia's waist and walked her to one end of the two-by-four. "All the way across. With your eyes closed."

Give the Lady a Ride

"Closed?"

He grinned. "It's only a two inch fall. Won't hurt you."

"Piece of cake," Marie said.

"Yeah, uh-huh. Piece of cake."

Talon planted a boot on one end of the board while Patricia stepped onto the other. Frank and Buster stood on either side of her, but neither reached up to steady her.

She closed her eyes and took the first step.

"Stretch your arms out for balance," Talon said. "There you go. Next step. Just walk."

Her legs wobbled as she tried to walk heel to toe. Feeling herself list to the right, she bent forward at the waist, then swayed backward and almost fell. Her eyes popped open. "Let me try it again."

She moved slowly, angling the arch of her foot across the board this time, using the balls of her feet or her heels to compensate for left or right listing. She still swayed but was better able to adjust her movements.

"That's it." Talon said. "Now you're feeling it. Make those adjustments. Keep your balance. Feel it."

"You're doing it!" Marie sounded like a mother watching her baby's first steps.

Patricia didn't peek until Talon told her to stop, then she opened her eyes and found herself at the end of the board. Everyone grinned at her as if she'd just won the gold medal for gymnastics.

"Ready to ride?" Talon took her by the elbow and led her back to the pen.

Inside the chute, she followed the procedure once more, feeling as if this time she'd get everything right and make the eight seconds.

Bart kicked his way out of the chute and ran into the pen, with Patricia bouncing on his back all the way. He twisted left, and she leaned to the right from her waist, tightening her groin muscle to keep herself centered. He straightened, kicked again, and spun to the right. She moved her free arm forward, gripping with her left leg, her chin tucked and her eyes on the bull's head.

She heard the distant eight-second whistle over the clang of Bart's cowbell and the thud of his hooves in the dirt.

"Dismount! Dismount!" Talon yelled.

She opened her fist just as Bart gave one final kick, and flew over his head, landing on her side in the dirt. Chance pulled her up and ran to the chute with a grip on her waist, lifting her to safety when they approached the rails.

She looked up at Talon and found his eyes shining.

"You made the eight."

Her lips twitched into a smile. "I did, didn't I?"

"Ready to do it again?"

Her legs felt like Jell-O and ached like she'd never known they could. Her riding arm was killing her, and her stomach felt like lead. If only she could get her heart to stop echoing in her ears . . .

"Maybe later, okay?"

With her sore muscles eased a bit after a hot bath, Patricia concentrated on her empty stomach. Since she had missed supper, she assumed she was alone in the house. She wanted to rummage through the refrigerator, then tackle the mound of paperwork in the office. After all the excitement of riding, she hadn't done anything she'd intended to do when she came to Texas. One of the first things on her list was to look for Uncle Jake's important papers.

She shook out her damp hair and studied herself in the mirror. If her hairdresser could see her now he'd scream out every expletive in the French culture. Funny how she didn't care anymore.

She dropped down the stairs, surprised to hear voices in the kitchen. When she turned the corner, she fell immediately under Consuela's scrutinizing gaze.

"Another late-comer." Consuela tsked. "Sit down, *muchacha,* and I will fix a plate." She winked at Talon, who was sitting next to her at the kitchen table, and hefted her bulk from the chair. "You'd think I was running a diner around here."

Talon had eaten halfway through his meatloaf and mashed potatoes, which looked so much better than the sandwich Patricia had in mind. She took a seat at the table and muttered a thanks to the older woman.

"Feel better?" Talon asked.

"Definitely."

"It's been reheated." Consuela put a chipped plate in front of her and sat down again. "You should get here on time. It would taste better."

"Sorry." Last week, Patricia would've seethed at Consuela's tone. Now, she just squirmed and searched the table for the silverware.

"Utensils are in that drawer." Talon pointed with his fork,

amusement sparkling in his eyes. "Glasses are there, ice is in the freezer, and tea's in the fridge. You need to learn your way around."

"Yeah, yeah." Patricia rose from the table, glaring at him with mock anger. "I don't even know my way around my own kitchen."

Consuela scowled. "Then you should learn that instead of bull riding. Learn something useful to a woman."

"Don't mind her." Talon patted the woman's hand and grinned. "She's just opinionated."

"Opinionated." Consuela twisted her lips and shot him a look. "What does that mean?"

Talon laughed. "It means you're sticking your nose where it doesn't belong. Again."

She huffed at him and went to the sink.

Patricia sat down with a fork and her iced tea, and dug into the meatloaf like she hadn't eaten in a week. In fact, ever since she arrived in Texas, she'd sat down to every meal like she hadn't eaten in a week. This southern cooking was heartier than what she ate at home, and if it weren't for the fact her clothes still fit, she'd believe she had gained ten pounds. Must be all this fresh air and exercise.

"Chef and Consuela are grilling at the Steak Cook-Off tomorrow," Talon said. "If you're not coming with us, you'd better eat your fill tonight."

"I saw the ads for the cook-off in town. It looked like fun."

"It's fun for the kids." Consuela twisted from the dishes she was washing. "It's just a whole lotta work for me."

Talon took his plate to her. "You love it. You know you do."

"I love it like I love the corns on my feet."

Give the Lady a Ride

He planted a kiss on her cheek, then grabbed a handful of sugar cookies out of a ceramic jar shaped like a worn boot, and returned to his seat beside Patricia. The smile he gave her made her feel that maybe Marie was right. Maybe she did belong here–belonged with him. Giddiness filled her as she gazed at that lopsided grin she was learning to love.

Consuela cleared her throat with theatrical effectiveness, and Patricia caught a glint of disapproval on her face before the old woman stretched a smile between her cheeks. "So, what you think? You coming tomorrow?"

Patricia returned her gaze to Talon and saw the expectancy in his eyes. "Of course, I'm coming. I'd never turn down a good steak."

"You won't be getting a *good* steak." Talon straightened in his seat and puffed out his chest. "Chef and Consuela grill the *best* steaks. Better than best–the greatest!"

"Oh, no you don't!" Consuela skewered him with a stern glare, waving a soapy spoon at him. "Every year you sneak a bite. Not this time!"

Talon winked at Patricia as if she understood the joke. "We'll see."

"I must go." Consuela wiped her hands on a towel. "I leave the dish water for you, *muchacha.* You know how to wash a plate?"

Patricia bristled. "I think I can manage it."

"Good. You ought t' learn to cook too." She folded the towel and placed it on the counter, delivering a pointed look at Talon. "Time for you to go. This is *her* house now."

Her husband appeared at the door and spoke sharply to her in Spanish. Her dark skin reddened and she smoothed her hands down the front of her apron. "*Sí, si,* I'm sorry. It's not my business."

Patricia watched her hurry from the kitchen. All the way to the front door, Consuela caught more angry words from her husband, and snapped her responses right back at him.

"I think she hates me."

Talon shrugged. "Consuela's not capable of hating anyone. I guess she's being protective."

"Of what? And from whom?" She shook her head. "No, she hates me."

He reached over to rub her shoulders. "Nah. You're too likable. Don't let her get to you. You'll win her over in no time."

She warmed under his hand and his gaze. Had she been standing, she'd be as wobbly-kneed as she had been after riding Black Bart.

His eyes darkened and his neck began to flush. He slowly drew his hand away, leaving her shoulder strangely cold, and cleared his throat. "So, uh . . . Do you want to go? You know, tomorrow? I mean . . . uh . . . with me?"

"Yes." Her voice sounded husky, and she cleared her throat too. "Yeah, sure, I'd like that."

Chapter Fourteen

Under the short scrub oaks at the Texas Steak Cook-Off, Patricia raised her nose to sniff the air. Smoke rose from cast-iron barbecue pits of all shapes and sizes. The tantalizing, spicy scents made her mouth water. "Smells like heaven."

"Nothing better than prime Angus beef grilling over mesquite." Talon studied the people around the pits for a moment. "There's Chef and Consuela."

He took her hand, interlacing their fingers as if it were the most natural thing in the world, and walked with her toward the pits. She smiled, relishing the casual intimacy, the feel of his strong, rough hand in hers, and the tingling warmth such a simple act sent coursing through her veins.

Chance and Marie caught up with them, and Chance flashed a toothy grin at Talon. "You thinkin' what I'm thinkin'?"

"It's tradition, man. Time to beg!"

Patricia sent a questioning glance to Marie, who shrugged as Chance whisked her away.

"We can't let them get ahead of us." Talon tugged Patricia

along.

"Wait, I can't walk that fast. I'm short, remember?"

"Can't let that stop us."

He scooped her up in his arms and jogged with her until they passed Chance, who shouted, "Hey, no fair!"

Patricia clung to Talon's neck and laughed out an *excuse us* every time her feet brushed an innocent bystander. Talon put her down in front of Chef's opened barrel pit, then circled around until he stood beside the short Mexican.

Chef closed the pit lid. "Uh-uh, not this time."

"Please?" Talon held his clasped hands to his chin and gave him a look Charles Dickens would've loved. "You know how I crave your steaks."

Chance joined him. "I'm so hungry. I haven't eaten in hours!"

Marie draped an arm around Patricia, laughing at the men's pathetic pleas and Chef's twinkling eyes.

When Chef planted his feet wide before the pit and crossed his arms over his chest like a storefront Indian, Chance turned to Consuela. "*¡Mama, por favor!*"

Talon took her hands and covered them with kisses. "*¡Tengo hambre!*"

Consuela laughed at them, her generous belly jiggling. "You can't be *that* hungry. We fed you a huge breakfast before we left."

"And you set aside a sample steak for us too, didn't you?"

Sending a wink to Patricia and Marie, she nudged past her husband and opened the pit. "Every year, these two. Every year!"

With a pair of tongs, she pulled a four-ounce steak from the back of the pit, placed it on a paper plate, and handed it to Chance. "All four of you have to share until after the contest."

She beamed when the boys kissed her cheeks. "Here, take utensils. You can't cut it with your teeth."

After the last bite, Patricia smacked her lips. "If the rest of their steaks taste like that one did, Chef and Consuela are a shoo-in."

She slipped her hand into Talon's as they walked. Chance and Marie had disappeared somewhere, so she had him to herself. "You called Consuela 'Mama'?"

"Yeah. Chance and I had a lot of moms while we were growing up. Consuela has four kids of her own, all grown and gone now. She was our after-school-snack mama. Frank's wife, Margie, was a mom until she passed away. She would mend whatever clothes we ripped and alter what didn't fit right. But Mama Loretta was queen bee. She had discipline rights the others didn't have."

"Like chasing you around the house with a broom?"

He smiled. "Among other things–yanking our driving privileges was the worst."

A booth of leather goods displayed purses, belts, and wallets. A tooled belt with turquoise inlays caught her eye, and she dragged him to the booth. Breathing in the savory scent of rich leather, she bee-lined to the belt display.

"This would match one of the shirts I bought the other day." She pulled the belt from its hook, wrapped it around her waist, and frowned. "Too big."

"Hey, Wilson." Talon shook hands with the vendor. "You got

Linda W. Yezak

this in a smaller size?"

"Don't think so, but I bet I could make one." The silver-haired Wilson flashed her a friendly smile, revealing a chipped tooth. "Just step around here so I can get a measurement."

As she skirted the display table, Patricia eyed a lady's wallet with a tinted yellow rose. She'd get it too, to commemorate her stay in Texas.

Wilson pulled a measuring tape from a small box on the table.

"Just don't say the number out loud." Patricia laughed as she raised her arms.

"Always discreet, ma'am." He took the measurement, holding his thumb on the tape to mark the size. "Nothing to be embarrassed about here."

"Nothing to be embarrassed about, period," Talon said.

Patricia glanced over her shoulder and flushed at the appreciative look in his eyes.

"How long will it take to make a belt?" he asked.

"Depends on my supplies and backlog." Wilson rubbed the stubble on his jaw. "Give it a month, six weeks at the most."

"In the meantime, bag this for me." Talon picked the rose wallet from the table and handed it to him. "I think someone likes it."

She was impressed he'd even noticed. Men and shopping generally didn't mix. Men being *observant* while shopping– that was unheard of. She crooked her finger at him, inviting him to bend down, and rewarded him with a light kiss on the lips. "Thank you."

He tipped his hat and gave her a look that made her heart flutter. "Worth every penny."

Give the Lady a Ride

She couldn't remember Kent ever curling her toes with a glance or making her giddy. But at this moment, with her eyes locked on Talon's, she could barely remember Kent at all.

Talon took her hand and they strolled to the edge of a crowd listening to a local band. From Patricia's left, a feminine voice shouted, "Talon!"

A tall brunette waved for his attention, and his face lit when he saw her. "Katie!"

The two hugged and Patricia stepped back to fight a wave of jealousy.

As they approached, Chance released Marie's hand and opened his arms. "Katie, how long has it been?"

"Too long, honey, too long." Katie wrapped him in a hug too.

Patricia stole a glance at Marie, who showed only curiosity—not the arousal of the green beast yawning to life in Patricia's stomach.

"Marie Lambeau, Pat Talbert, this is Katie Pierson, former barrel racing champ and unofficial bull rider," Chance said. "And my favorite kid sister."

"Mine too." Talon's eyes shone with fondness for her.

"I don't understand," Patricia focused her confusion on Chance. "I didn't know you had a sister."

"Rodeo family." Katie wrapped an arm around each man and beamed. "Horsehide kinfolk."

"You must be pretty close, then."

"Not just close. *Family.*" Katie filled the word with conviction. "I've known these two since we rode stick horses in our backyard rodeos."

"You ride bulls?" Marie glanced at her slender body. "You

don't look strong enough."

Katie laughed. "Strength isn't everything. Balance helps."

"Patricia is learning all about balance, aren't you?" Pride and affection shone from Talon's eyes, and Patricia warmed under his gaze. "She'll be the next lady bull riding star before you know it."

"Well, great! I'll be able to say I knew you when." Katie's smile was all teeth and sparkle, and held no hint of anything other than happiness to meet the friends of her two horsehide brothers. Patricia returned the smile and began to relax.

"Hey, what're we standing around here for?" Chance said. "They're judging the steaks now."

"Chow time, folks!" Talon draped an arm around Patricia's shoulders, and once again she felt cloaked with a warm sense of belonging.

Give the Lady a Ride

Chapter Fifteen

At the first taste of her steak, Patricia had let out a low appreciative sigh, and even with her stomach filled to the brim, she couldn't help bemoaning that only one bite remained. Seven people sat at a tree-shaded picnic table meant for six. She was nestled between Talon and Marie, with Chance as the fourth on her bench; Frank and Buster flanked Katie on the opposite side.

"Chance said you were a *former* barrel racer." Marie eyed Katie over her plastic tea glass. "Why did you quit racing?"

"Had a bit of an accident at my last event."

"Scared us all to death." Buster rubbed her back in an affectionate gesture that marked him as part of the horsehide family. "A lot of praying went on that night."

"What happened?" Patricia asked.

"A few years back, I entered a race against my dad's advice. He warned me about the poor conditions in the arena, but I ignored him. I loaded my best horse and went off to the rodeo."

"You rode Percy then, didn't you?" Talon asked. "Good-looking sorrel."

"Yeah, he was my baby. Anyway, Percy and I were tearing up the track around the barrels. But the sand was wet. Coming around the third barrel, Percy's legs flew out from under him, and I fell off. He landed on top of me. Cracked a couple of my ribs and snapped my collarbone. He broke his leg and couldn't get up."

"Not that he didn't try," Buster said. "He was panicked and flailing his legs. Had us all scared."

"And every time he moved, I felt something else break. I finally passed out."

"I don't believe I breathed for an hour seeing you down like that," Talon said.

"I don't think anyone was breathing," Chance added. "It was like all the oxygen had been sucked out of the arena."

"One of the top equine vets in the area was in the stands that night. He grabbed his bag of tricks and sedated the horse, stabilized the leg." Frank steepled his arms over his plate and finished Katie's story. "They rolled Percy off her and whipped her to the emergency room 'fore you could say *Jack Spratt*. Had to pull Percy out of the arena with chains and a pickup."

"Chains?" Patricia pictured the poor injured horse with heavy logging chains wrapped around him, being dragged across the sand.

"He was sedated, ma'am. Unconscious." Frank told her. "It was the only way."

"Did they have to put him down?" Marie had always been tender toward animals.

Katie gave her an understanding smile. "No, hon. They fixed him up, and he was almost good as new in a few months. But he can't race anymore."

Give the Lady a Ride

"What about you?" Patricia reached for her tea. "What happened with you?"

"I stayed in the hospital for a while with a broken collarbone, a couple of broken ribs, and a collapsed lung. Everyone on the circuit came to see me, but these guys– " Katie glanced around the table, looking at each man through misty eyes. "They were with me the whole time. They'd switch out, take shifts, but at least one of them was with me 24/7 until I went home." She focused on Patricia. "That's what I meant when I said we're family."

"Yes, I can see that." Patricia's throat tightened as she watched Frank pull Katie over and plant a fatherly kiss in her hair. A different kind of jealousy heated Patricia's chest. Very few among those she considered friends would drop everything for her. What would it be like to be part of a group who didn't look at her as a means to an end?

When the orange sun dropped below the hills, strands of white lights outlining the ancient storefronts snapped to life. With a flick of some unseen switch, the town's short, dusty main street became a fairytale city.

A different band had set up on the small stage. The leader stepped to the microphone and called, "Cotton-Eyed Joe!"

"Time to dance." Talon grabbed Patricia's hand to pull her from the bench.

She stayed planted where she was. "I don't know how to do this."

Marie let Chance haul her to the street. Buster and Katie rushed to the crowd arm in arm. Only Frank and Patricia remained seated.

"It's the easiest dance in Texas. I'll teach you." Talon gave her arm another tug and she allowed him to pull her up.

Everyone on the street lined up, four to six people dancing shoulder to shoulder, arms wrapped around their neighbor's waist. Patricia smiled up at the Flying K's owner, Ben Kilgore, as he offered his arm to invite her into the line.

"Hook your fingers through my belt loop," he said. "It'll be steadier."

Patricia wrapped her middle two fingers through the loop on the back of Ben's jeans while Talon instructed her.

"Kick your right leg forward and bring it back, step backwards three times. Then we'll do the same on the other foot. Right, left, right, then we'll skip–you'll see."

Patricia watched her feet and stumbled through the steps. More than once a heavy boot landed on her toes, and just as often she landed on someone else's. She grew frustrated; she was a good dancer in New York's ballrooms and clubs, never lacking confidence on the polished floors.

Where did you come from?
Where did you go?
Where did you come from,
Cotton-eyed Joe?

The lines moved forward with a set of stutter-steps while Patricia was still stepping back. She regained her balance and got it straight just in time for the next set of kicks. By the third repetition of the song, she was kicking and skipping with the best of them. The band upped the tempo with each round until everyone was dancing at a frantic pace and laughing so hard they could barely hear the music. At the last few notes, Talon swirled her away from Ben and dropped her into a dip, then pulled her up for a hug.

"I told you it was easy." He seemed as breathless as she was.

"I feel like I've had a workout."

The band slowed the pace with "Waltz Across Texas." Talon led her into the three-quarter beat, rubbing his thumb along her spine. She knew the proper posture for a ballroom waltz, but this wasn't a ballroom. Resting her cheek on his muscular chest, she allowed herself an inward sigh as he led her in slow turns around the street. With her eyes closed, she could pretend they were the only two dancing, not on the street, but in the clouds with the star-glittered heavens above them. They moved together with an ethereal grace until the final note. Applause rumbled from the crowd and jerked her back to earth, but she lingered in his arms a moment longer. He seemed as hesitant as she to break the spell between them. As everyone disbursed, she reluctantly pulled back and gazed into his eyes, finding them dark and enticing.

A polka beat fired up, and Katie tapped her shoulder. "Mind if I have this one?"

Yes, she *did* mind, but she dug up enough grace to step back and smile, casting a final glance at Talon. He shot her an apologetic look even as he opened his arms for Katie and whirled her away in time with the music.

Patricia edged back to the spectators, but never took her eyes off Talon and Katie. Few of the street dancers could match their practiced expertise. They moved in unison as they whipped around the turns. Talon pushed her out to twirl under his arm before pulling her to his side and continuing the steps hip to hip. With another twirl under his arm, Katie was facing him again and they swirled into another set of turns.

"That's been their dance for years," Frank said from beside her. "Won a contest with it once."

"*Really?*" Talon was in a dance contest? She shifted her eyes to Frank's leathery face. "Why aren't you dancing?"

"Bum knees." His faded blue eyes lit. "You forget I'm old."

She linked her arm with his. "Not too old to buy a lady a drink?"

They walked to the refreshment stand where she asked for a bottled water and kept an eye on Katie and Talon. They looked good together. Katie was the right height, coming up to his nose instead of barely reaching his chin like Patricia did.

Family or not, Patricia couldn't release the jealousy she felt while watching them. They fit together too well, were too at ease with one another. Five years ago, she'd missed all the signs with Kent. She would not make that mistake twice.

Talon slammed the truck door and shoved his hands in his pockets as he walked Pat to the ranch house. He hesitated to reach for her hand. She'd been quiet on the ride home, didn't even wait for him to open her door and help her from the pickup. She didn't seem angry, just . . . upset somehow.

His stomach tightened as they approached the porch; he wasn't ready for her to go inside. "It's a nice night. Feel like taking a walk?"

"I'm a bit tired." She shifted the sack bearing the rose wallet to her left hand and reached into her pocket for the house key.

"We could sit out here for a while." He waved toward two oak rockers flanking a small table on the porch and flashed her his best *aw-shucks* grin. "I'll even let you have the one with the cushion."

She rewarded him with a light laugh and pushed the key back into her pocket. "How very chivalrous of you."

He rested a hand on her back and guided her to the chair, hoping to find a way to get her to confide in him. It was unfamiliar territory to him, prying into another's thoughts, but he needed to know what was wrong. "Well, now you know the whole family."

"No more mothers lurking in the woodwork?" She placed the sack on the table and took a seat. "No more brothers and sisters?"

"That's it. But I'm glad you met Katie." He dropped into the rocker and rested an ankle on his knee. "We're close. I've known her since before my parents died."

She fidgeted with the sack. "I wasn't sure what to think of her."

"You weren't sure what to think of her? Or of me?"

She rose, walked to the porch rail, and leaned out to look at the waning moon. After a few moments, she said, "Kent and I met at a fundraiser. It was a special night—my first time helping with my dad's campaign and my twenty-first birthday. I guess I was a little starry-eyed." She faced him, her arms wrapped around her waist. "He swept me up in a whirlwind romance. We were married within three months."

"How did he die?"

"Drunk driver caused a three-car collision in five o'clock traffic. His was the middle car."

A lump formed in Talon's throat. She was too young to be a widow. Softly backlit by the mercury light near the pens, her hair was an angelic gold. She was so tiny, so beautiful. He wanted to fill pages of his journal with poetry for her. About her.

"I loved him. And I thought he loved me." She brushed a strand of hair from her eyes. Her voice took on a hard edge he hadn't heard before. "But he'd had four other women in the first year we were married. I stopped counting during the remaining three years."

Talon's eyes slammed shut. Anger roiled in his throat, and he clenched his teeth before he interrupted her with his unfavorable opinion of her late husband.

"Just before he died, I filed for divorce. That's when he told me he had only married me to get next to my dad. He figured the senator's career would be good for his own."

"The man was an idiot." Talon shoved to his feet and crossed the narrow porch to stand before her. He rubbed his hands along her arms. The tightness in his throat made his voice gruff. "You deserved so much better."

"Yes, I did." She tilted her head, lifting her chin to show him defiant eyes. "I still do. But thanks to him, it's not easy for me to trust anymore."

"No, I don't imagine it is." Words formed in his mind and tumbled out to his tongue before he could reconsider what he was about to say. "I'd like to try to earn that trust. I know Chance has asked Marie to stay. Will you? Will you give me the opportunity to earn your trust?"

She regarded him for what seemed an eternity. The lump in his throat grew and threatened to choke him. Was he tempting God, running the risk He'd allow another love to disappear from his life? Or was she the one he was to wait for? He didn't know. He just knew he wanted her here. Wanted to know her, to love her.

Give the Lady a Ride

She turned from him to look again at the sky, and he winced. He had rushed her. She'd probably catch the first plane home. But he couldn't take his words back now. Maybe he should let her know he was in no hurry. She could take her time, he'd wait. He started to speak, but kept silent when she faced him.

"You're not through teaching me to ride," she whispered.

The breath he'd been holding released in a rush. "Is that a yes?"

"It's an 'I'll think about it.'"

"You're lucky she's still here," Frank grumbled from the bunkhouse porch. "You almost blew it, boy."

"Who're you talking to?" Buster stepped out and caught sight of Talon. "Oh, you're back. Did you and Ms. Talbert make up?"

Talon scowled. "Does *everyone* know my business?"

"When it includes the boss lady, your business *is* everyone's business," Frank growled. "She watched you dancin' with Katie tonight like she was watchin' her life slip through her fingers. She's only known you a week, and she don't know Katie at all. How was she supposed to figure there's nothing between you two? Didn't you think she might get jealous?"

Talon plopped on the top step and leaned against the post. "Did she say something to you at the dance?"

"She doesn't even know I noticed, son. She wouldn't say anything anyhow–she's a lady."

"Yeah, she is." And no longer a New York lady. She was country gentility. She belonged here. With him. "I asked her to stay."

145

"What did she say?"

"That she'd think about it."

"Well, if she does decide to leave, maybe she'll just give you the ranch." Buster headed back inside. "The plan might be working even if your romance ain't."

"She gets mad at him again, she ain't gonna be givin' him nothin'–not even another cup o' bad coffee." Frank shoved to his feet. "You need to stick to the plan. Get that woman to like ya."

"I'm working on it." A window closed back at the main house, and Talon turned in time to see the curtain move. "Anyway, this isn't about the plan. I really want her to stay."

"I know." Frank rested a hand on his shoulder. "You love her. If you don't believe me, just ask yourself how you'd feel if she did give you the ranch, then high-tailed it back to New York."

It was too early to admit to love, but Talon didn't have to ask himself how he'd feel if she left. His heart already shriveled at the thought.

The plan? Patricia backed away from the window, her hand at her throat. The words had wafted to her on a soft evening breeze, turning the air sour and cold.

Was all of Talon's attention part of a plan?

She backed into the bed and sat heavily near her pillow, which she grabbed and hugged to her chest. The artificiality she thought she'd left behind in New York was everywhere. Everyone masked their agendas in rehearsed smiles and tepid affection.

And she'd been fooled again. Would she never learn?

She retrieved Jake's letter from the bedside table.

146

Give the Lady a Ride

I want you to have the Circle Bar . . . The people here are real and honest and good in a way you may not have found in the big cities. If you stay and work on the ranch for a while, learn the ways of the good folks around here, your education in life will be complete.

Jake's words sounded sincere, and Loretta's love for the men around here also seemed sincere, as did their affection for her. Apparently the people here were real, honest, and good only to their own.

In that respect, they were no different from anybody else.

Chapter Sixteen

"Get up, lazy bones." Marie pounded on Patricia's bedroom door, then entered unbidden. And stopped at the threshold. "What are you doing?"

Patricia slapped another bundle of clothes into her almost-full suitcase. "I'm leaving, and if you're going with me, you'd better get packed."

"I don't understand. Why are you leaving?" Marie crossed the room and took Patricia by the shoulders, turning her away from her task. "What happened?"

"Nothing happened." Nothing she was ready to discuss. She shrugged away from Marie's grasp. "I've just neglected my responsibilities long enough. And so have you."

"But I thought you were going to buy some time. I thought we were staying for awhile." Marie lowered herself on the bed, pushing aside the tangled sheets which evidenced Patricia's restless night. "Did you and Talon have a fight?"

"No, we didn't fight." Not at all. Fighting wasn't part of the plan. But Talon saying he wanted her to stay, wanted to gain her trust–*that* was part of the plan. And she'd almost bought into it.

After a few moments of watchful silence, Marie said, "Chance wants me to meet him at church this morning."

"You would do well to just forget about Chance and come back with me." She plopped a garment bag next to Marie and unzipped it.

Marie grabbed her hands. "It's obvious you're angry about something, and you're taking it out on me. At least you can tell me why I should put up with it."

With a tired sigh, Patricia settled on the foot of the bed. Although the focus of her anger was a toss-up between Talon for fooling her and herself for allowing it, Marie didn't deserve to bear the results. But Patricia just wasn't ready to discuss it. She glanced at her friend who was clad from head to toe like a rancher's wife–pink broadcloth shirt, paisley scarf and all. "You're wearing blue jeans to church?"

"It's a cowboy church. Casual. And I want you to come." Marie went to the closet and withdrew a pair of Wranglers and a burgundy cap-sleeved blouse.

"Can't you just get a ride with the men?"

"They've already left. It's their turn to set the place up." She waggled the clothes on their hangers. "Please come with me. It's important."

"Why? What's going to happen?" Marie was so smitten with Chance, she may have been up to something crazy. Were they getting married after all? Could they get married on such short notice? Surely not. Patricia's eyes narrowed. "What do you have planned?"

Marie's eyes brightened like sunlight through quartz. "You'll see."

Give the Lady a Ride

Patricia studied her, yet couldn't discern what she was hiding. But after being such a bear this morning, Patricia felt she owed her friend this request. They could always leave after church. Besides, maybe she could stop Marie's impetuosity in whatever form it revealed itself. "Oh, all right. Give me a few minutes to get ready."

Marie squealed and piled Patricia's clothes on the bed. "I'm going to get something to eat while you get dressed. Hurry, okay? I don't want to be late."

Patricia watched the door close, once again alone in the room. Was Marie's attraction to Chance part of the plan too? Should she be warned before it was too late?—or was it already too late?

No, Marie didn't own the ranch. Patricia did. The plan was aimed at her and designed for Talon and the others to keep their jobs. And if that was all he wanted, she'd ease his mind.

She dressed quickly and slipped Jake's letter into her hip pocket.

Before the service, the sand at the rodeo arena had been smoothed and the bleachers cleaned. In the center of the arena stood a makeshift dais, complete with a podium, microphones and amplifiers, and potted Gerber daisies. Sitting with Marie and Katie on an aluminum bench halfway up the stands, Patricia studied the congregation. All around her sat men, women, and children of all ages, all casually dressed in denim—jeans, skirts, jumpers. Women not wearing denim wore western broomstick skirts and silver jewelry. Patricia fit in like she belonged. Too bad she didn't.

On the dais, Talon rose from one of two metal folding chairs and strode to the mike. Chance followed, stopping just long enough to pick up a guitar from a stand and strap it over his shoulder. Soon, Talon was crooning "The Old Rugged Cross" in a smooth baritone. Chance strummed his guitar and angled toward the microphone at the chorus, joining his tenor in harmony.

The song was one of Patricia's favorites, and as always, it brought a lump to her throat. When she was twelve, her parents had taken her to a Billy Graham Crusade. There, squashed between her parents on a hot night, she'd heard the song for the first time.

She could no longer remember the sermon, just the way she'd felt after it–like her eyes had been opened. That night, she had accepted the Lord along with thousands of others, only to discover that her soil was rocky and the seed hadn't rooted. Now she didn't know where she stood with God.

After the final notes faded, Chance put his guitar back on its stand and took a seat on the stage. Talon retrieved a book and returned to the podium.

"Open your Bibles, if you would please, to the third chapter of Proverbs. I want to take a good look at verses five and six."

Talon was full of surprises. He had never once told her he could sing or preach. But his Christian facade didn't fool her. He would stoop to dishonesty to get what he wanted–just like so many others she knew. The thought brought a bitterness to her tongue.

Closing her ears to him, she studied her hands. Each of her previously manicured nails had broken at least once since she'd started riding, and a tender, red callus stretched across her right palm from grasping the bull rope. In New York, she wouldn't have allowed her hands to degenerate into such a state, but here, she hadn't cared. She'd earned that callus, and the broken nails didn't seem as important to her as the sense of accomplishment she'd gained while breaking them. At least she'd have that to take home with her.

But she almost dreaded going back to New York. So much of ranch life appealed to her, just as Jake had hoped. The simplicity, the easier pace. She didn't know where she belonged anymore. Not in the brutal civility of the political world, but certainly not here where the schemes were just as vicious.

"'Trust in the Lord with all thine heart, and lean not unto thine own understanding.'" Talon's deep voice resonating through the speakers pierced her thoughts. Her eyes snapped back to the stage. "'In all thy ways, acknowledge him and he will direct thy paths.'"

A chill shimmied down Patricia's back. She half expected to see Talon looking straight at her as if he were reading her mind and advising her.

"The way I see it, you can't go wrong if you follow the instructions in this passage. Trust the Lord. Talk to Him. Tell Him what's weighing on your mind. He'll lead you the way He wants you to go. And His way is always the right way. Always what's best for us, even if we don't think so." Hooking his thumbs through his belt loops, he leveled a gaze at the crowd. "God loves us. He'd never lead us wrong. We just need to trust Him and wait on His guidance."

Trust in the Lord. How wonderful it would be to receive His guidance while her future seemed dim. But how was she to find His will? She didn't even know where to start.

At the end of his sermon, Talon issued an invitation for anyone wanting salvation to come forward. Marie jumped to her feet as if spring-loaded and made her way to the arena floor. Patricia's eyes grew wide as she watched her friend's pink cotton shirt approach the platform.

Chance's face split with a grin, and he rushed down the platform steps to meet her. He wrapped an arm around her shoulders and tilted his head toward her. Marie swiped a finger across each of her cheeks. Her lips moved in animated speech. Chance nodded his head and patted her shoulder while she spoke.

Patricia couldn't see herself doing what Marie had just done, rushing before a large crowd to make a confession so intimate. Her religion was her business. She didn't need an audience.

She backpedaled from the thought of *her* religion. Hers was so stagnant it reeked. Even if she tried to find His will, how could she expect Him to help her?

With his arm still around Marie, Chance turned to the stage and motioned to Talon for a microphone. Looking as jubilant as Chance, Talon handed him the mike and clapped him on the shoulder.

Chance faced the congregation. "Folks, this is Marie Lambeau, a very special friend of mine. Marie just told me she wants to give her life to the Lord and be baptized."

The arena exploded with applause and a boisterous chorus of amens. Marie ducked her head in uncharacteristic shyness.

Chance grinned. "Nice to see I'm not the only one whose face turns red."

In the ensuing laughter, Katie slid over on the bench and sat closer to Patricia. "That's wonderful, isn't it? Does this mean

Give the Lady a Ride

y'all've decided to stay in Texas?"

"No." Patricia shook her head. Had Marie decided? "I mean, I don't know. If Marie is staying, she didn't tell me."

Would Patricia have to return home without the only friend she trusted?

Chapter Seventeen

tanding at the entry gates to the arena, Patricia watched Marie emerge from a denim sea of huggers and hand-shakers. By the time she caught up with Patricia, she was flushed and glowing as if she'd just accepted a marriage proposal in Yankee Stadium.

"I'm so happy for you!" Patricia reached out to give her another hug to add to her collection. "What made you decide to go up front?"

Stepping into the embrace, Marie gave her an enthusiastic squeeze. "Chance did. He's been talking to me for a while now. Hasn't Talon discussed God with you?"

"A little. He assumed I was already a Christian."

"And you are."

"Not a good one." She retrieved her keys from her purse and started toward the car. "What did Chance say to make you change your mind about public displays of faith?"

Marie slowed her pace and looked at Patricia. A sense of wonder shined from her eyes, and she squinted, as if trying to find the right words. "It wasn't so much what he said, but the way he said it. Like he was humbled, and grateful, and joyful all at once. I've never met anybody who talks about God the way he does."

Patricia nodded. From her own experience at the Billy Graham Crusade, she remembered the feeling of awe. As the years went by, she'd lost it. But she'd felt it again when she read Loretta's letters, felt inspired by a faith so strong as to pull her aunt through the death of her children. She craved that same feeling of security in the arms of One who understood her and was capable of healing all her hurts. Could she reconnect with God here on the ranch? Return to the faith she'd neglected so long ago?

Talon's plan wasn't important any longer. What mattered was regaining her faith, and she was determined to figure out how.

She unlocked the car and prepared for the drive home.

"I'm getting baptized next week, and I want you to be there." Marie slipped her seatbelt on. "Are you still planning to leave?"

"No, not yet." She straightened, pulling her shoulders back, and sat tall in her seat. "I'm going for a ride."

"She sure looks good on a horse." Chance watched Pat and Tandy through the dining room window as they turned down the trail by the horse barn and headed into the valley.

Feeling uneasy, Talon watched her too. She seemed to have been avoiding him. Hadn't spoken to him at church, hadn't waited for him after. He'd searched the crowd for her and found her sitting with Marie and Katie, studying her hands. If she'd ever even looked at him, he hadn't seen it.

Give the Lady a Ride

Marie entered the room, out of her Sunday jeans and now in a pair khaki walking shorts. Chance appeared to forget all about Pat. "Here's our new sister in Christ. We've got you ready for the horse trough now."

"Horse trough?" Marie slid onto the bench beside him and smiled as he slipped his arm around her.

"They didn't tell you about the horse trough?" Frank raised a brow at Talon. "Don't you reckon you oughta warn th' girl about that?"

Buster winked at her. "It ain't nothin', Ms. Marie. I'll make sure they scrub it out good for ya. Keep the horseflies at bay."

"I don't understand. What's the horse trough for?" Marie's puzzled expression made it hard for Talon not to break out laughing.

"Don't let them tease you, *muchacha*." Consuela lumbered in from the kitchen with a steaming tamale casserole and a bowl of salsa and placed them on the table, then sat down. "Everybody gets baptized in the trough. It's clean. No horseflies."

"Texas horseflies won't fit in it anyway. Trough's too small." Chef brought in the tea pitcher and sat at the end of the table next to Buster. "Don't know why we don't catch a few of 'em and ride 'em in the rodeos."

"I'm too scared of them," Talon said.

Marie eyed him. "Let me get this straight. You're going to baptize me in a horse trough?"

"That's the only way we can do it." Chance passed his plate to Consuela for her to fill. "There isn't a good place in the river nearby, and the creeks are too shallow."

Marie's eyes danced. "Patricia's going to be glad she decided not to leave when she hears this!"

Talon almost dropped the plate he was passing. "Why would she be leaving?"

Marie scowled at him. "I was going to ask you the same thing. Did you two have a fight last night?"

"No. I mean, not really." He received his plate from Consuela who studied him with tight lips.

"*Not really*? What does that mean? Either you did or you didn't."

"We didn't. We had a . . . misunderstanding. I thought we straightened it out last night." He turned to Marie. "Did she say anything to you?"

"No. She seemed fine last night, but this morning I found her packing her bags."

Talon's heart withered in his chest. Maybe he *had* rushed her by asking her to stay. Maybe after being married to a jerk like Kent, she wasn't ready to risk another relationship.

Frank stroked his mustache. "I'm just wondering, was that her that closed the window last night while we were talkin'?"

"Yeah, she's in my old room . . . oh, no. You don't think–?"

Frank's brows rose over narrowed eyes. "Reckon you'd better figure out what's goin' on."

Talon was halfway out of his seat before Frank finished his sentence.

Patricia needed to ride all the thoughts out of her head. She kept a loose hold on the reins as Tandy picked his way down the hill. When they reached level land, she urged him to a gallop. She felt at one with him; her body moved in rhythm with his. She needed this. The wind through her hair, the motion of the ride. The cattle grazed in the far pasture, so she had this one to herself. She aimed Tandy at a downed log and laughed out loud as he flew over it. That instant–that flash of time when she was suspended in mid-air, with the horse's body stretched out beneath her–was the most liberating feeling she knew. And Tandy could vault over a fence as well as any of her show horses.

She slowed him to an easy walk, draped the reins around the pommel, and rode with her arms raised over her head. With her eyes closed and her chin tilted toward the sun, she let the horse take her to her favorite pond. Was this what leaving all her burdens to God felt like? Riding with the sun on her face and not worrying about a thing? How wonderful it would be to have a relationship with Him again.

A calf's frenzied bawl nearby drew her attention. She reined Tandy to the left, kicked him into a trot, and skirted around a stand of cedar trees. Across the fence from her, a small white-blazed calf struggled against the barbed wires tangled around his head and foreleg. His hind legs slipped under him as he twisted to pull himself free. He stretched his neck and let out a cry, which his mother answered with an anxious bellow.

Patricia bolted from Tandy's back and wrapped his reins around a cedar branch. She paused beside the fence, took a deep breath, and compelled herself to calm down before approaching the animal.

While studying how the fence was wrapped around him, she eased up to the calf. "Poor baby, you're in a bit of a mess, aren't you?"

The bottom and middle wires had wound taut around him, the bottom wire below his neck and the middle above it. A thin line of blood oozed across the calf's throat. His right foreleg, raw from its injury, had twisted between two lines next to his head. Rolling panicked eyes toward her, he kicked at the dirt, twisting his head and crying frantically until his legs went limp and he sat on his haunches like a puppy.

The sight of the terrified baby too tired to fight tugged at Patricia's heart. She shoved a boot on the lower wire and raised the upper wire, feeling it dig into her hands. Her actions tightened the lines around his foreleg and he screamed with pain. She eased the tension on the wires and stumbled back, running her hands through her hair.

There had to be some way to set him free. She walked the fence line until she was far enough away from him she could climb over without hurting him, then circled back. Keeping a wary eye on the cattle—and especially the mother cow, which swished her tail and paced several yards away—Patricia edged up to the calf and squatted in the grass beside it. She eased the wires from his foreleg just far enough so he could jerk it free. Once again on four feet, he wrestled against the lines wrapped around his neck, wrenched his head, and pulled free with what strength he had left. He released a final bellow and tottered to his mother's outstretched nose.

Patricia squatted by the fence and watched until the calf curled into a ball in the grass. His mother returned to her grazing with the other cattle nearby, all cause for concern passed.

Behind the massive trunk of a live oak, Talon slouched on Sable with his arm resting across the saddle horn, and watched Pat. The McAllister blood must've run thick in her veins. The way she had rescued that calf was all rancher. No city girl would've dirtied her hands like that or risked cutting them on the wire. Watching her wrestle with the fence to free the calf warmed his soul. Did she realize how much she'd changed since coming here? Did she realize how much she belonged on the ranch?

He clicked his tongue, and Sable walked toward the fence where Pat crouched watching the calf.

She looked up at him and nodded toward the animal. "He was caught in the fence. I got him loose, but I didn't know what to do. The poor thing struggled until he was just too weak."

"Good thing you came along." Talon dismounted and pulled two fence lines far enough apart to step through and join her. "Just last year, we lost a calf in the fence. Strangled to death."

He gave her a hand up and walked with her toward the cattle. As they approached, the calf jumped and bolted. Talon darted to the right and caught him, then carried him by the flank and brisket back to where Pat stood.

"Yep, this little fella was lucky you came along to save him. You're like his own personal savior."

Her lips curled up. "That's me, the matron saint of cattle."

"You going to give him a name?"

She tilted her head, regarding the fence marks around his neck and foreleg, then laughed. "I think I'll name him *Wireless*."

Talon grinned. "That works." With a grip on the calf's ear, he ran a hand along the foreleg, then twisted the animal's head up to get a look at the scratch on his neck. The injuries weren't deep, so he swatted the calf's rump and watched him scamper away. "Cowhide's tough. He's going to be fine."

"To hear him cry from that fence, I thought he was dying." She watched him nudge his mother's udder and greedily begin to feed. "He sounded so pathetic, but he does seem better now."

Talon watched her watching the calf. Had she heard them

talking about her last night? About the stupid plan that no one took seriously? Frank had probably come up with the idea just to throw Talon and Pat together. After all, he'd noticed the attraction between them even before Talon was willing to acknowledge it.

It didn't matter whether Frank devised the scheme to hang on to the ranch or to play matchmaker, the result was the same. Pat must've heard and misunderstood. There was no other explanation. The thought of her leaving tore at him. He gritted his teeth against the questions rising to his tongue. There was an art to nosiness, and he was certain he didn't have the talent for it. He usually left everyone's personal thoughts alone and expected the same in return. But this woman's thoughts affected his life, his future. He needed the knack for prying.

"Did you enjoy your ride? I mean, aside from finding a panicked calf."

"Oh, yes." The shine in her eyes reflected her pleasure. "Anytime I'm on horseback, I'm enjoying myself."

"I know how you feel. I get a lot of my thinking done when I'm riding. Praying. Talking things over with God. Nothing like an afternoon ride for that sort of thing."

"Do you pray often?"

"Yeah, I do. It's a major part of my life."

"Do you believe God hears you?"

"Wouldn't waste my time with it if I didn't."

She sighed and returned her gaze to the calf. Talon wanted to wrap his arms around her, relieve the thoughts that furrowed her brow. Instead, he shoved his hands in his pockets and plunged headfirst into nosiness. "Marie said you were packing this morning."

"I was, but I changed my mind."

"Want to talk about it?"

"No." She lifted her chin in that defiant way she had. Last night, he'd been proud to see it, proud she'd survived the ordeal of her marriage and come out stronger. Today, the look made him uneasy. "But I will say this: You can stop pretending you're interested in me so you can get the ranch. I can settle your mind about that right now."

She yanked a folded paper from her hip pocket and shoved it at him. He accepted the sheet and opened it to see Jake's familiar block lettering. *Dear Pattie, First time I laid eyes on you, I figured there was nothing more beautiful . . .*

He skimmed the letter, still surprised Jake and Loretta had kept silent about their blood relatives all those years. His own name in the last paragraph caught his eye.

> *If you stay and work on the ranch for a while, learn the ways of the good folks around here, your education in life will be complete. But if you decide to leave, do me the favor of letting the boys, Talon and Chance, have it. I'd rather you gift-deed it to them but if not, give them an honest price and carry the note. They're good for it. Either way, Pattie, try to keep all of my men together. This is their home. I want them to stay.*

The breath he drew whistled through his teeth as he reread the lines. Jake had thought of them after all. He'd done what he could to assure they had a place on the ranch.

A memory played in Talon's mind of the night he'd found Patricia crying in the kitchen. He tapped the letter lightly against his palm. "Is this what you were reading the other night?"

"Yes. I'm sorry. I should've told you about it much earlier. After I'd read this and discovered I had an alternative to selling the spread, the question came down to whether I wanted to keep it or give it to you." Her lips tightened. "After last night, it's become much easier to make up my mind."

Talon winced. "I think I know why. You heard us talking, didn't you?"

"Yes! Talking about the *let's make the woman fall in love* plan so you and your men can keep your jobs and home here." She glared at him. "Well, it's all yours! I'll get Jake's attorney to draft a gift deed tomorrow, and as soon as Marie gets baptized, I'll be on the first plane out of here."

"You misunderstood. I don't want you to leave." At that, she snorted and turned away from him, but he snatched her arm. "Let me explain–"

"Explain what?" She yanked herself free. "That you're no different from the men I know in New York? That you won't think twice about using me–hurting me–to get what you want? I've had enough of that. At least when I get used back home, it doesn't take me by surprise. But I thought you were different." She swung away and stalked to the fence and her horse on the other side.

"Wait, it's not what you think." Talon raced to catch her shoulder and turn her to face him. "Would you just listen to me?"

She crossed her arms and stared at the ground. Her anger throbbed under his fingertips, and he knew the strong emotion would drown his words before they reached her heart. He rubbed her shoulders gently and said, "Come walk with me."

Chapter Eighteen

With a sullen shrug, Pat followed Talon. It was a good sign. Maybe she didn't really want to believe the worst of him. Maybe she was willing to hear him out and give him another chance. Question was, how on earth could he explain *the plan*? The way she'd had it figured was precisely how anyone else would have: get the woman to fall in love to save the ranch. Whether or not that was the way the idea had started, it wasn't what he felt now. Not that he was in love with her—it was too soon for that—but he'd like to see whether what he felt would develop into love.

He stopped beside a weeping willow next to the pond and prayed that God would direct him and give him the words he needed to reach her. Stooping down, he grabbed a pebble and skipped it across the water. Stiff and distant beside him, Pat wrapped herself in her arms and watched as the two rings in the water grew and intersected, rippling until at last the surface was calm again. Talon sifted through the pebbles, finding another smooth one, and tossed it. Again the two rings collided.

"You see that?" He looked up at her, but she remained focused on the pond. "We're like that. You and I rippled toward each other and merged on a course I'd like to see to the finish. We'll either have a smooth pond together, or we'll have rough waters and have to part ways." He stood and took her by the shoulders, peering into her face until she returned his gaze. "Only God knows how it'll be. I just know how I feel, how deeply I've come to care for you in such a short amount of time. I don't want you to go. I want to see what God has in store for us."

Uncertainty replaced the hostility in her eyes. "How will we know what God wants? How will *I* know?"

"Ask Him. Wait for His answer." He turned to where Wireless was sleeping in the tall grass while his mother grazed. "The cattle on this ranch are our responsibility. We're God's responsibility. We look after the herd to protect our profit, but we're lucky. God looks after us because He loves us."

"I've neglected Him for so long, I'm a stranger to Him. Why would He take the time to answer my prayers?"

"You took the time to answer a crying calf. Why wouldn't He take time to hear you?" He wrapped her in his arms and filled with joy when she returned the embrace. "No one's a stranger to Him. Just bawl like that calf in the fence and see if He doesn't listen to you."

A sweet night breeze billowed the curtains as Patricia unpacked her garment bag, but no voices rode it through her window this time. That Talon hadn't tried to explain the plan made her believe her impression was right, but the sincerity in his eyes when he told her he wanted her to stay was unmistakable. Whether she could trust him–could trust her judgment of him–would be determined over time. For now, she just wanted to enjoy the ranch and seek the faith her aunt had possessed.

Marie appeared at her door with a knowing smile on her lips. "Where were you all afternoon?"

"With Talon. We had a good talk."

"What did you talk about?"

"Things." Patricia slid the garment bag under the bed and started on her suitcase.

Marie sauntered into the room and plopped on the bed. "You're not being very forthcoming. Do I have to dig it out with a spoon?"

"You're not going to give up are you?"

"Nuh-uh. Give." She rubbed her hands together. "Did he kiss you?"

Patricia rolled her eyes and grabbed her clothes out of the suitcase.

"Okay, okay." Marie huffed. "You don't have to tell me."

"Thank you." She loaded her lingerie into a dresser drawer and counted to herself. *Three, two* . . .

"I can't stand it!" Marie jumped from the bed and pulled Patricia back to it. "You have to tell!"

Patricia fell, bouncing on the mattress and laughing. "He didn't profess his undying love, if that's what you want to hear."

"But?"

"But . . . he wants me to stay."

Marie squealed and wrapped her in a tight hug. "Chance and I were hoping you two would work it out. What did you say?"

"That I'd think about it."

"So, what do you think?"

"I don't know, Marie. I need to think about it." She laughed again and gave Marie a quick squeeze before rising. "So you and Chance have talked about us? What did he say?"

"That he hadn't seen Talon so smitten in years."

Patricia stopped halfway to the dresser and turned. "*Years?*"

"Chance says Talon doesn't get involved too often." Marie's voice turned serious. "He thinks everything started when Talon's parents died in the fire."

"Did he tell you about that?"

"A bit." She shifted her weight on the bed, pulling her legs under her. "He said Talon was eleven when he lost his parents and a couple of pets in that fire. He'd managed to escape out the window and tried to get back in to save his parents, but a fireman held him back. He watched the fire consume the part of the house his parents were in."

Patricia slowly lowered herself onto the bed and clutched a pillow to her chest.

"He lived with his grandmother for a while, but she died soon after his sixteenth birthday. After that, he just started withdrawing." Marie twisted around to face her. "Jake and Loretta took him in and pulled him out of his shell. But a few years later, Loretta died. And when Katie had her wreck in the rodeo soon after, Talon all but shut down. It was just one thing after another for him."

"That's a lot to endure. So many deaths to deal with."

"And it's not just that. Talon's only had three loves in his life. The first was a childhood crush, but the girl's family moved to California just before high school. Then, his senior year, he fell for another girl. They went off to college together, but she changed so much he had to break up with her."

Give the Lady a Ride

"You said there were three. What about the third?"

"Chance wouldn't tell me about that one." She picked at some lint on the sheet. "The way he clammed up, it must've been painful."

"Poor Talon." Biting her thumbnail, Patricia cast her eyes to the window. Heavy boots climbed the steps below and crossed the wooden porch. Soon, there was a knock on the door.

"That's Chance." Marie jumped from the bed. "We're going to Stephenville for a movie tonight. Want to come? We can get Talon and make it a foursome."

"No, not tonight. I'm going to finish unpacking. Do some thinking."

Marie hugged her. "If you come to a decision, I want to be the first to know."

"Same here if you come to one."

She watched the door close behind Marie and continued to stare at it. She ached for Talon. He had lost everyone he loved–almost lost his childhood friend too. To see Katie injured must've been agonizing for him. Yet he continued to go to church. He prayed after every ride. Maybe before the ride too. Was that Jake and Loretta's influence? Had he found the faith they seemed to possess? What would it be like to have such a strong trust in the Lord?

Clad in a striped pullover, stained jeans, and boots, Patricia descended the stairs at five thirty the next morning with a light step and followed the smell of sausage and the sound of masculine laughter to the dining room. After her experience with Wireless, she'd decided to learn what she could about ranching while she was here—work with the animals, spend her days on horseback. Although she'd prayed before going to bed last night, God hadn't answered her yet; but if He decided she should return to New York, at least she'd have a new experience to share at parties.

"You should've seen her. She's a natural for ranching. I hope she decides to stay."

Talon's voice halted her steps at the dining room door and brought a smile to her lips.

"Ain't her ranchin' you're impressed with," Frank drawled, earning the laughter of the other men. "But I hope she stays too. She's spunky. Got gumption. I like that in a woman."

Chance caught sight of her in the doorway, cleared his throat, and nodded in her direction as if to signal the others. As she entered the room, the men rose and stood at attention—knights before their queen. From the kitchen door, Chef and Consuela grinned with the amusement of a shared joke.

Patricia narrowed her eyes, hesitating at the door. Had she surprised them by actually waking up in time for breakfast? Maybe she'd done something wrong to cause them to revert to formality.

Or was this western etiquette?

A grin flickered under Frank's mustache. "Welcome to our humble table, St. Pat."

Her lips twitched. Fitting greeting for the Matron Saint of Cattle.

Straightening as tall as her small frame would allow, she glided into the room with a tilt of her chin and a Queen Elizabeth wave to her worthy subjects. Chance hurried from his place on the bench, bowing with his hands held prayerfully at his chin, then pulled out the seat at the head of the table. With regal grace, she lowered herself onto the white-painted chair with its worn, red cushion, and raised her hands to tap at the air, allowing her loyal vassals to return to their seats.

And that was as far as she could go with the charade before cracking up. "You guys are crazy, you know that?"

Buster slid a platter of pancakes to her. "Been told a time or two."

She helped herself and glanced around the table. "What's on the agenda for today? Anything I can do?"

Silence and a couple of suppressed grins met her question, so she focused on Talon. "You're the boss. How can I help?"

"It's up to you." He sipped from his mug and eyed her from over the rim. "You can ride the tractor with Frank while he cuts hay. Or, you can go heat detecting with me and the rest of the hands. Your choice."

"Heat detecting?"

His dark eyes were inscrutable, but something in his tone had her squinting at him with suspicion. She flicked her gaze to Chance. His neck glowed brilliant red as he struggled to keep a straight face.

She focused again on Talon. "That isn't similar to wild goose chasing, is it?"

"Sometimes."

She crossed her forearms on the table. "Finally. Something I'll be good at."

Give the Lady a Ride

Chapter Nineteen

In the dawn's pastel haze, a white pickup rolled to a stop on the gravel drive in front of the horse barn. Buckling the cinch on Tandy's saddle, Patricia eyed the two men who emerged from the truck and recognized them as the ranch hands she had yet to formally meet. One was a sliver of a man, sinewy and tan, dark wavy hair peeking out from under a John Deere cap. The other, a stocky redhead with an uncovered military burr-cut, was peppered with freckles. Both were in their early twenties. She led Tandy out and introduced herself to them.

"Pat's doing your job today, Jack." Talon came up from behind her and handed her a clipboard with a multi-paged chart and a pen dangling from its beaded chain. His gaze remained on the dark-headed Jack. "Saddle up Pacer so you can help Randy with the cutting."

As the young men left to get their horses, Patricia studied the papers Talon had given her. The title, "Post-partum Interval Records," was typed across the top of the page followed by columns of dates and numbers. Looking over the column headings, she began to understand what *heat detecting* meant.

"We're going to see if the cows are in heat?"

"Yep." Talon grinned. "A job we've neglected since you got here."

"And for that, we thank you." Chance led a piebald mare from the stable and tossed her reins over a fence rail. He walked to Patricia's side, shoved his hands in his hip pockets and let out a dramatic sigh. "But now we must return to real life and all the duties it involves."

"Well, if you want me to help with those real-life duties, you'd better clue me in how to do them." She tapped the PPI chart and focused on Talon. "Just so you know, I refuse to sniff rumps."

"Then you're in the wrong business, lady. There's no other way."

She shot him a wry smile.

Chance waved Talon's comments aside. "Aw, he's just pulling your leg. You don't really have to sniff the rumps. But you do have to sneak up on the cows." He crouched and duck-waddled a few feet before turning around again, holding a thermometer he'd retrieved from his shirt pocket. "Then slip this up under the tail and check their temp. Won't be easy."

Patricia twisted her lips. Her baloney meter was shooting through the roof, but it was impossible to determine whether he was joking. Chance's blush was usually a good indicator, but this time no color rose in his neck.

He jumped to his feet. "Let me warn you, they may resist this procedure."

"That's right." Talon took it from Chance and tapped it in the air as a warning to her. "You have to be careful not to get kicked."

Give the Lady a Ride

She wrinkled her nose. Surely they were kidding her. Pulling one over on the city girl. Getting their laughs at her expense. Surely.

Neither man cracked a grin.

Twenty minutes later, Patricia and the five other cowhands scattered grasshoppers as they rode down the hill. The sun in front of them glowed soft yellow in a pink and blue haze. In the southern meadow, beyond the horse pasture, Frank rounded a corner with the tractor, mowing the hay behind him. Cattle dotted the pasture where Patricia had found Wireless the day before. Many of those cows were nursing calves. They couldn't already be in heat, could they?

Her stomach roiled at the thought of having to find out. She would do it, probably grinding her teeth the whole time, but she would do it. Allowing the men to have a laugh at her expense riled the daredevil in her, but she still didn't know whether they were telling the truth. If it *was* the proper method, then Aunt Loretta had done it. And if Loretta could do it, so could she. She hoped.

Once the ground leveled beneath them, Talon turned Sable and waited for Patricia to catch up. "Jake had an old-fashioned way of doing things. The PPI clipboard is just a relic from another era. These days, there are computer programs that help with record keeping."

Patricia smirked. "First you need a computer."

"You noticed that, huh?"

"I also noticed that Consuela does the dishes by hand and all the phones in the house are attached to a cord." She rolled her

179

eyes toward him. "I think *old-fashioned* about sums it up."

His eyes took on the hopeful gleam of a five-year-old at Christmas. "Then you'd be willing to update some? Bring this ranch into the new century?"

She gave him a sardonic smile. "Does the ranch make that much money?"

They stopped the horses in front of the pasture gate and waited while Jack leaned down from his bay mare to open it.

Once everyone had ridden through and the gate was locked behind them, the men split up and walked their mounts around the herd. Chance hummed a tuneless melody as he and Buster ambled south to a knot of cattle by the pond. Randy and Jack eased northward to the hillside, leaving the middle of the pasture to Talon and Patricia. Talon lined up next to her and reached for her hand. She wrapped her fingers around his.

"Are you *really* going to make me crawl up to the cows?"

"Naw. We were just having fun."

She heaved a sigh of relief, swiping a theatrical hand across her forehead and winning a chuckle from him. "So, how *do* you tell if they're in heat?"

"There's signs you can watch for. Behaviors, physical indicators."

The cattle lumbered away as they neared, but Talon's quick eye caught the tag number of a cow he said was pregnant. Patricia wrote it in the margin of the chart.

Another, grazing apart from the herd, caught her attention. "What about that one?"

Talon twisted in his saddle, his lips twitching when he saw the animal she meant. "That's a steer, ma'am."

"Oh." Sucking in her bottom lip, she wondered how many

shades of red there were, certain she'd blushed them all. To his credit, he didn't laugh, but she wouldn't have blamed him if he had.

A half-hour slid away as he pointed out signs and called numbers for her to record. Work on the ranch was relaxing. She could put in a hard day and never once come home tense from having to juggle schedules, placate egos, or deal with the rudeness inherent in her job back home.

Talon pulled Sable up beside her again and maintained an easy gait toward another group of cows.

"Ever think you'd be doing this?"

"What? Horseback riding with a handsome man while studying the bovine reproductive cycle?" She slanted a glance at him. "Always been a dream of mine."

The sound of his laughter delighted her. What it would be like to hear this richly masculine sound every day of her life?

Remembering what Marie had told her about his past romances, she asked, "Ever been in love before?"

He reined to a stop. "That question's out of the blue, isn't it?"

"Touchy subject?"

He squinted at the horizon, lost for a moment in his thoughts. When he turned, his focus was on something just beyond her. She cringed at the deep pain in his eyes, sorry now she had asked.

"Janet. Her name was Janet."

The gruffness in his voice jolted her. She dared not say anything further and was unsure how to lighten his mood again. Whoever Janet was, she'd left a wound still raw in Talon's heart.

"We have to round up the cows and herd them down to the pen." He clicked his tongue and trotted off to the south, without a second glance at Patricia.

At a loss, she yelled to him. "What do I do?"

He tossed his response over his shoulder. "I'll go this way, you go that way. Get 'em all."

She watched him circle behind the farthest cow and ease it toward the group, sweeping out to get another and aim it in the same direction. Touching a heel to Tandy's side, she rode north to do the same.

The cows had a mind of their own. She'd get one going the right way and when she went after another, the first would mosey off to a grassy patch in the opposite direction. She tried to get the two wayward animals moving toward the herd, while keeping an eye on a third meandering farther away. Should she go after it or come back for it? She had no way of knowing and didn't dare ask.

She decided to go after it, nudging Tandy to sweep wide around it and come up from behind. Watching the two she'd just abandoned stop to graze, she pushed the third toward them. As she neared, she rounded behind those two and got them moving again. She concentrated on bringing the cows to the herd and tried not to think of the pain she'd brought to Talon.

All these years and the thought of Janet still rocked him. Would the pain *ever* go away? Would Janet's memory destroy every chance for a new love, for happiness in his life? He could still see her dark, chestnut hair and bright hazel eyes–eyes that had promised a lifetime of love–and his heart clutched with loss.

Give the Lady a Ride

He knew he needed to move past it. His feelings for Pat, growing stronger with every passing day, gave him hope that God didn't mean for him to be alone forever.

What kind of a jerk was he to ride away from her as he had? He should've stayed and told her everything. But the question had taken him by surprise. Still, she deserved better from him. He watched her from across the field. For a novice, she was doing a great job. She walked Tandy back and forth behind three cows, keeping them all in line and heading for the bulk of the herd midway between her and Talon.

Teasing her this morning had been fun. She was a good sport for a Yankee. He needed to retrieve the levity they'd shared. As his four cattle converged with her three, he offered her a smile. "You're a born cowgirl."

"You think so?" She slipped a wayward strand of hair behind her ear, studying his eyes with an unnecessary apology shining from her own.

"Well, you didn't run away screaming the first time a cow said moo. I reckon that's a good start."

She rewarded him with saucy grin. "If I wasn't going to be afraid of getting on a bull's back, I certainly wasn't going to let a cow scare me."

"As long as you didn't have to sniff her rump?"

The sound of her laughter eased the tension. "Right. And thank you for not making me touch her tail."

"Never said you didn't have to touch her tail. Soon as we get the pregnant cows separated from the estrus ones, we're going to palpate them."

Her face turned a nice shade of pale green. "Palpate?"

By late morning, Talon had Pat's arm in a long plastic sleeve, secured at her shoulder with white medical tape, and was helping her lubricate it.

"Are you sure I can do this?" Her face scrunched up with obvious distaste.

"Of course you can. You've been paying attention, haven't you?"

"I've been watching, yes. But what do I feel for?"

"You'll know."

He had specifically chosen Tilly for Pat. Most of the cows in the pen required an experienced hand, but this one was at least five months pregnant, relatively safe for a novice to palpate with a high possibility of feeling the calf.

Once the sleeve was gooped up all the way to her shoulder, he turned her toward the back of the squeeze chute—a chute specially designed to minimize the cow's movements. The men stood wherever they could best see her face, expecting a good show.

"What's going on out here?" Marie, looking shower-fresh and well-rested, climbed to the top fence rail and balanced on it.

"Pat's going to palpate a cow." Chance jumped onto a rung and gave her a swift kiss. "If you weren't such a late sleeper, you'd be doing it too."

"*Palpate.* Does that mean to . . ." She shifted her gaze to the plastic sleeve on Pat's arm, then back to Chance, taking her answer from his mischievous grin. "Uh-uh. Really. No thanks."

"You don't know what you're missing," Pat called.

"She really doesn't." Talon ignored the sarcasm in Pat's voice and stationed her at the rump bar behind the cow. "This is quite an experience. She'll be jealous she missed her chance."

Give the Lady a Ride

"Yeah, right." Pat tossed him a lackluster grin.

He laughed. "Ready?"

She squinched her nose. "This has a pretty high *ew* factor. You know that, don't you?"

He patted her back. "You'll be rewarded for your efforts. Trust me."

"I'm trying to." As she followed his directions, her scrunched nose gave way to concentration for a few moments. Then her eyes brightened. "I feel him! He moved!"

"How big is he?"

"Maybe the size of a cat? Maybe a big cat–He moved again!"

Marie jumped into the pen and was by her side in a shot. "I want to feel it."

"Sorry, one cow per customer," Talon said. "But I'll see if we can find another for you."

Talon strode to another pen to survey the remaining cattle and issued orders about which one to cut out.

Patricia grinned at Marie. "That was amazing. He's so tiny!"

"Is it really gross?"

"Yeah, a bit. And the muscle contractions are so tight I thought she'd squeeze off my circulation. But you forget all about it when you feel the calf." Wrinkling her nose again, she carefully peeled the plastic sleeve from her arm. "Ranch life is messy. I was telling myself that the whole time. Ranch life is so messy."

From a cardboard box wedged between two corner posts, Chance whipped out a clean sleeve for Marie. "You're going to find out first hand, huh?"

Patricia laughed at Marie's wobbly grin. "I felt the same way.

But really, it's worth it."

The honk of a horn drew her attention to the gravel drive behind them. Katie jumped down from a black pickup and jogged to the pen, her brown hair bouncing in its ponytail. Patricia choked back a wave of territoriality. It was one thing to run into the woman in public, quite another for her to welcome herself here.

But Katie wasn't the threat, if Patricia could believe Talon. If Janet were to ever return, Patricia would be in serious trouble. Besides, Katie was special to everyone on the Circle Bar. No point alienating her.

She offered a smile and a wave.

Katie waved back and crossed the pen to join them. "Guess what! Ben's entering his three-year-olds in this weekend's rodeo."

Chance lit up as if it were his birthday. "He raises some great buckers. I need to pay up and ride."

Talon returned and clapped Chance's shoulder. "We didn't get to see the threes buck the other day, but if his babies were any indication, you know we're in for a good time."

Buster cleared his throat. "You boys reckon you ought to practice some?"

"Wouldn't hurt." Talon twisted around to shout at Randy and Jack. "You two need to–"

"Let me guess." Randy grabbed the reins on his dun and lifted himself into the saddle. "We need to haul in the bulls and steers for y'all to practice on."

"That's why I like ya, Randy." Talon grinned at the redhead. "Always on top of things."

Chance draped an arm around Katie. "You want to ride one

while we practice?"

"It's been a while." She glanced at Patricia. "But I will if Pat will."

Patricia hesitated just long enough to read the woman's eyes. Katie was issuing an invitation, not a challenge. If she truly had no designs on Talon, Patricia could like her as a friend. She gave her a warm smile. "Sure. But keep in mind, I'm not very good."

"Now if we can just get Marie to try." Chance shot her a grin.

"Nuh-uh. No way." Marie peeled the plastic sleeve off her arm. "I can't even believe I almost tried this."

Patricia giggled. "You are such a city girl."

"Yeah. So, what's your point?"

Chapter Twenty

"Stupid straw," Patricia muttered as she climbed the rail to drape her legs around Black Bart. She had hoped to go *after* the others–not first. Not with everyone watching her. Even Chef and Consuela had parked their truck near the tiny arena to watch from the tailgate.

"Relax, you'll do fine." Talon rested his hand on her vest. "You remember what to do?"

"I remember."

Bart snorted and shifted his weight as she strapped her hand in. Resting her free hand on the rail, she waited until he settled again, then worked her way to his shoulders.

She nodded at Randy. "Pull it."

Randy pulled the gate open, and Bart ambled out of the chute, glancing around at the people watching him. Had he been capable, he would've said *ho-hum*, scratched his belly, and reached for a soda.

"Kick him," Talon called from behind her.

She jabbed at him with her heels as hard as she could, but he just swung his head back as if to brush off a fly and meandered to the grass in the corner.

Frank blew the eight-second whistle, and Chance cupped his hands around his mouth. "Folks, we have our first qualified ride of the night! Everybody give the lady a hand!"

The small group whistled and cheered, making her laugh. She loosened her hand from the rope, slid off Bart's back, and waved her hat as if she'd just won the prize buckle. Then she trotted to the fence to sit with Marie and Katie. "I'm going to be tough to beat."

Katie gave her a hand up. "If we were in a real rodeo, they'd offer you a re-ride."

"I can do that? I can have a re-ride?"

"Don't see why not."

"Then I want one." She called to the chute, "Frank, I want a re-ride."

"We'll have a steer left. You can ride that one after everyone else."

Talon straddled the rails, sliding his glove on before he entered the chute. "I can't let you ride a steer yet. They're wilder than the breeders."

"Let me try. Please?"

Frank said something Patricia couldn't hear, and Talon nodded, then climbed into the chute.

Patricia studied Talon and Chance as they each rode in turn. Watching them from a few feet away instead of from the stands, she was able to see the almost imperceptible shifts in body weight to adjust to the movements of the steers beneath them. Neither man had an impressive ride, not like in the rodeo, but she used this opportunity to learn from them.

As Jack and Randy herded Chance's bull out of the pen, Katie dropped from her perch on the fence and jogged to the platform behind the chute.

"You go, girl," Patricia called. "Show the guys how it's done."

"Now we'll see some action," Marie yelled.

Katie tossed them a smile and a thumbs-up as she climbed the steps to the platform. She bounced from one foot to the other, shaking her arms to keep them limber. When the steer was in the chute, she climbed over the rail and onto his back. A few seconds later, she gave the nod.

The striped steer bolted from the chute and, after kicking the air, settled into a left spin. Katie struggled to stay on. Her steer was the only one of the evening willing to put on a show. When the animal reversed his spin, she flew off and landed in a heap just below Patricia and Marie. She jumped the fence and watched over her shoulder as Randy rushed the animal, chasing him out of the pen.

"Seven point six seconds," Frank called out.

"Well, that stinks," Patricia said. "The only exciting ride tonight wouldn't have qualified."

Marie draped an arm around her. "Makes the rest of you look a bit wimpy, doesn't it?"

"Says the one who won't ride at all." She dropped into the arena and marched to the platform steps, where she confronted Talon. "Can I have a re-ride?"

"Frank talked me into it." He waved her up to the platform. "The flank strap makes them buck harder, so we'll just leave it off to give you a fair shot. But keep in mind, that steer is wild. Even without the strap, he can be dangerous."

She nodded, but her stomach fluttered with butterflies.

A black and white steer as big as Bart entered the chute. Jack slid the back gate closed just as the steer snorted and jabbed a hind leg, making the rails ring.

The butterflies in Patricia's stomach morphed into crows. She must be out of her mind.

Talon frowned at her, concern clouding his eyes. "You don't have to do this if you don't want to."

She stared at the bull slamming around in the chute. Would she wimp out in front of everyone? In front of Talon? In front of Katie, who could ride better, dance better, fit in at the ranch better? She liked Katie, but just this once, Patricia wanted to be the better one.

She lifted her chin and smiled at Talon. "Let me at him."

The steer twisted his head toward her as she climbed in. His muscles tensed when she draped her legs around him. He shifted his weight, pawed the ground.

She stopped breathing.

If her colleagues in New York could see her now, they'd reserve a padded room in Bellevue just for her.

The steer snorted, and she grimaced. Maybe it wouldn't be so bad to spend the day hugging herself in that cute little jacket.

"Ready?" Jack stood on the chute gate, braced to pull the bull rope.

She situated her hand and nodded.

The steer shifted again as the rope tightened around him. His tail flicked.

Patricia clenched a rail, and her teeth. To steady her nerves, she sucked in a chest full of air through her nose, breathing in the stench of the steer's dirty hide. Then, only marginally fortified, she wrapped her hand and worked her way to the bull's shoulders.

Lord, please. Let me do this.

She raised her free hand. "Pull it!"

The gate jerked open, and the steer raged from the chute, flinging his rump and bellowing. Patricia flew off and landed on her shoulder a few feet from the gate. As soon as she jumped to her feet, she scrambled from the pen. The bull rope had fallen from the steer, and he stood snorting in the center of the arena.

Frustrated with her performance, Patricia shot a glance at Talon. "One more time?"

Buster chuckled. "Girl loves to ride, doesn't she?"

"Run him to the chute, Randy," Talon called. "Last time, Pat. I'm hungry."

The platform planks softly thumped under her weight as she bounced from foot to foot and watched the steer reenter the chute. She rolled her left shoulder. It was sore, but her riding arm was fine. She drew her lips tight. This time she'd do it. "All right, *Mostro*, let's try again."

"*Mostro*?" Talon asked.

"Italian for *monster*." She glared down at the animal.

"Good name."

She climbed into the chute and readied herself.

"Pull it!"

The gate opened, and Mostro charged out into a bucking spin, nose to tail. Patricia landed on her back with a breath-stealing thud.

"That's it. We're done. Put up the gear," Talon yelled. "Dinner time."

Patricia rose slowly and slapped her hat against her thigh, scowling over her shoulder at Mostro as Jack and Randy chased him from the pen. She'd thought he would kick like the first time. She'd been unprepared for a spin.

Anticipation would land her in the dirt every time, Talon had said.

"Keep your head up," Chance told her. "You rode Bart for eight."

"Thanks, but a carousel ride would've been more challenging." She dusted herself off and slipped out of the pen to join Marie and Katie on their walk to the house.

"Always hungry, this group." Consuela eased off the tailgate and followed them. "We'll make tacos. Won't take but a minute."

In the kitchen, Consuela gave each woman a task, but she had to show Patricia how to shred the cheese. As they worked, Patricia's mind shifted from her pitiful ride to Talon's behavior earlier in the afternoon. With the two women who were closest to him in the same room, it seemed the perfect time to ask. "Does anyone know who Janet is?"

Katie's knife paused over the onion she was chopping. She cast a glance at Consuela, who regarded Patricia with suspicion.

"Why do you want to know?"

Unnerved by the look on the woman's face, Patricia fumbled the grater and flipped shredded cheese all over the counter. Heat rushed to her cheeks as she tried to clean it up. "He-he mentioned her earlier. I just wondered."

Consuela studied her a moment longer, then turned to stir the seasoned ground meat sizzling on the stove. After several unsettling moments, she said, "Janet was Talon's fiancée."

Patricia stared at the woman's back before shifting her gaze to

Give the Lady a Ride

Katie.

Katie resumed chopping the pungent onion, and her eyes began to tear. "He met her in college, dated her a couple of years before proposing. She was from Dallas and wanted to be married there, close to her family and friends." She scraped the onions into a bowl, then put the knife down and faced Patricia. "She was found in her car the night before their wedding. She'd been murdered."

Patricia drew in a sharp breath and fumbled behind her for a chair.

"What happened?" Marie sounded as stunned as Patricia felt.

"No one knows." Katie found a red bowl for the lettuce Marie was shredding and placed it on the counter beside her. "Talon was suspected at first. His name was in the news in Dallas and around here. He was in shock. Ashamed and embarrassed by all the attention. It took them forever to figure out he wasn't involved. The case has been unsolved for eight years."

Patricia brought a hand to her lips. She couldn't imagine Talon murdering someone. How anyone could even think it of him was beyond her.

"We don't talk about it around here," Consuela said. "When he came home, he climbed into his shell and hardly said a word to anyone for a year. Just went through the motions of living. Dark times. Dark."

Katie pulled out a chair beside Patricia and dropped into it. "When he visited me in the hospital–after my horse went down in the arena–we had long talks deep into the night. It was the only time he ever spoke of Janet."

"That poor boy has lost just about every woman in his life. Except Katie and me." Consuela turned with a fist on her ample hip and shook her spoon at Patricia. "He's got eyes for you now. You'd better make up your mind what you want to do about the ranch. About him. And make it quick. I won't stand to see him hurt again."

Patricia swallowed and nodded. "I've been praying about it."

"Pray harder."

Later in the evening, Patricia sat cross-legged on her bed, fingering the rough nubs on the cotton sheet. "Can you imagine what it must've been like for him to lose his fiancée *and* to be blamed for it?" She dropped the sheet and rested her back against the headboard. "That must've been horrible."

"Chance told me once he wouldn't leave the ranch because of Talon." Marie dropped on the bed beside her. "Said Talon had lost too much already. He didn't want to add to it."

"I thought Chance loved it here."

"He does, but his heart's in the ride. Given the opportunity, he'd rather be on the circuit."

Patricia gave her a wry smile. "Is that the life you want?"

"You don't have to worry about me," Marie said. "I know what I want. I've made up my mind. I just wonder what's taking you so long. You said you've been praying about it."

"I have been." She sighed. "How will I know when God has answered?"

"In my mind, He already has. You're just too stubborn to see it." She took Patricia's hand in both of hers. "I don't understand your indecision at all. You're one of the most decisive people I know. But, friend to friend, you're not being fair to anyone by dragging your feet. You love it here, and you love Talon. A blind man could see it."

"It's too early to say that I love Talon."

"Then give it a chance to develop." Marie's voice held a sharp edge of impatience. She rose from the bed. "You promised to pray about it. Pray!"

She left the room, closing the door behind her. Patricia flipped off the bedside lamp and drew her knees to her chin. Everyone was rushing her. No one recognized what a monumental decision this was. If only God would give her a sign—preferably in neon green.

Patricia Talbert, you are to remain on the ranch for the rest of your days!

That would be clear enough.

And if it wasn't too much to ask, she'd like to know what would happen between her and Talon. The fact that Janet's name still affected him was disturbing. How could she compete with a ghost? Could he ever love her as he had Janet?

The words to the old song, "Que Séra, Séra," entered her mind—*whatever will be, will be.* Her lips twisted into a frown. The song didn't offer a philosophy that fit her life at the moment. After Kent, she wanted to know where her foot would land before she dared to move it. Climbing out on a limb in faith scared her more than she cared to admit. She'd already fallen out of that tree once.

But Talon's laughter brightened her day, his touch warmed her, an intimate glance from his dark eyes curled her toes. She no longer believed he'd meant to hurt her with the plan.

She slid her legs under the sheets, brought the covers up to her chin, and stared at the dark ceiling. Everyone was right. She couldn't let this drag on forever.

Her mind traveled from Texas to New York, to Kent's snarling face five years ago.

"You're nobody," he'd said. "Without your father, you're just another little rich girl. He's the only reason I married you."

The words echoed in her head.

What crushed her was that he was right. Since her days of show jumping, she'd accomplished nothing without her father. She wanted to succeed at just one thing as Patricia Talbert, not as Senator McAllister's daughter.

Bull riding was beginning to symbolize the success she craved. Her father had nothing to do with it. He didn't even know she had ridden. The activity was pointless. It wouldn't change the world. But it could change *her* world. Facing her fears, making the eight, suddenly felt important to her.

But even if she *had* made the eight today, it wouldn't have meant anything. Katie had ridden her steer with a flank strap. Patricia's time on Mostro was the equivalent of riding a bike with training wheels. And falling anyway.

Had Talon figured her incapable of doing it? Did he, like Kent, see her as just another rich girl?

The thought raked over her mind like claws. If he didn't believe in her, why should she stay?

The clock's glowing red numbers oozed out one more minute, changing Monday night into Tuesday morning. Patricia watched another minute slide by, and another, with the foolish notion that if she lay still long enough, she'd fall asleep. When twelve-fifteen became twelve-sixteen, she untangled herself from the cotton restraints of her sheets and sat up on the bed.

Give the Lady a Ride

Hot milk. She'd never liked it, but it might work.

Slipping her robe over her shoulders, she stepped barefoot from her room and headed downstairs. Her mother used to make her warm milk when she was young. Patricia had hated it because it meant she would sleep through her opportunity to witness the nighttime activities of adults.

She snorted softly. She was an adult now, and her nighttime activities consisted of tossing, turning, and watching the minutes slip by.

On the main floor, instead of turning right into the kitchen, she turned left to the office. She flicked on the light switch, blinking at the assault on her eyes. Once they adjusted, she shifted them to the bookcase and found the one thing she should've consulted earlier. A Bible.

She eased it from the shelf and moved to sit in a chair in front of the desk. The leather scrunched and squeaked as she pulled her feet up under her and rested her knees against the arm.

The well-worn book smelled of dust and age. It sported a blue padded cover with an *ichthus* on the binder. Inside, she found the same fish symbol under Loretta's name, and her heart vaulted to her throat.

Loretta's Bible.

Patricia caressed it as if she'd discovered the Dead Sea Scrolls. Would Loretta ever have struggled with a decision such as the one plaguing Patricia's mind? Had she been able to find the answers to her heartaches in the pages of this book?

The Bible must've provided her with some comfort, something to hold onto during the times she mourned her children. Patricia's problem paled in comparison.

She let it fall open and read the first thing her eyes fell upon, verses from the seventy-third Psalm already highlighted in yellow.

> Thus my heart was grieved,
> And I was pricked in my veins.
> So foolish was I and ignorant:
> I was as a beast before thee.
> Nevertheless I am continually with thee:
> thou hast holden me by my right hand.
> Thou shalt guide me with thy counsel,
> And afterward, receive me to glory.

Her lips parted as she read. David's description of grief and vexation hit home. It was as if Loretta had opened the book to this particular place for her to see. No. Even better–God had. He knew of her inner turmoil and wanted her to know He was with her to guide her. She just needed to let Him.

She closed her eyes. "Please, God. You'll find me willing to do whatever You say."

Chapter Twenty-One

arly Wednesday afternoon, Patricia leaned back in the office chair as far as she could without tipping over, eased her gritty eyes shut, and rubbed her throbbing temples with both hands. She'd been studying the ledgers to the beat of the men repairing the barn roof. Occasionally she caught a glimpse of Talon's bared muscles as he hauled tin or swung the hammer, and she'd watch in fascination until he moved beyond her sight, then sigh and return to the books.

Her crash course in ranch management had her cross-eyed with fatigue. Every dollar earned and spent on the ranch, every asset, had a ledger: the house and outbuildings, vehicles and farm implements, the full- and part-time ranch hands, the livestock.

That was the killer–the *livestock!* Everything was recorded. Purchase and sale dates, corresponding weights for both, prices for both, including the auction's price-per-pound average on the sale date. Vet expenses, feed and supplement expenses. Supplies. Trucking fees for when hay had to be hauled in from out of town. Bovine medical records.

She squeezed her eyes tighter against the numbers swirling behind her lids. Never would she be able grasp everything. She was tired, cranky, and sick of the desk chair's flat cushion that offered minimum protection from its metal frame.

The phone rang, and she peeked at it. Not quite comfortable in her role as the owner, she had avoided answering the phones on the ranch. Talon was best for talking to whomever called, but he was on top of the barn. She grabbed a pen in case she needed to take a message and lifted the receiver.

"Circle Bar Ranch."

"Hello, sweetheart."

"Daddy!" Her father's voice washed away all her weariness. She glanced at the clock. Two in Texas. Three in DC. He was probably in his office. "I can't believe you could find time to call."

He chuckled. "So, how's everything going at the ranch?"

"It's a different world, but I'm learning to love it here. How are things there? Marcy still doing you good?"

"Oh, sure. She's a gem, but she's not you. Got the paperwork done?"

"Haven't made a dent." Patricia twirled a strand of hair around her finger while she eyed the insurance papers and bills she'd yet to look through. Twisting her chair away from the intimidating stack, she looked out the window. She should have called him after she'd made her decision early Tuesday morning, but worried about what he'd say to her news. She bit her lip. She may as well get it over with. "I found a letter Uncle Jake wrote me sometime before he died."

"What did it say?"

"That he was sorry for the distance between you. He just never knew how to apologize."

"Well, the distance wasn't entirely his fault. I should've called, shouldn't have let it drag on as long as I did."

"So you forgive him?"

"Of course. I forgave him long ago." Regret weighted his words, and he fell silent.

"Jake wanted me to stay at the ranch and get a feel of country life. He thought it would round me out as a person." She took a deep breath through her nose, releasing it through her lips. "What would you think if I stayed?"

He snorted. "You'd tire of it, Pattie. The novelty will wear off soon enough. It's hard work, even for the women."

"I'm learning that." She closed her fist over the calluses in her hand. "But I like the work. And I like the people."

He was quiet for a long moment. "Do you *seriously* want to stay?"

Moment of truth time. Would the decision she made during her hours of prayer hold up to her father? She snapped her eyes shut. "Yes. I do."

Silence roared in her ears. His office chair didn't squeak like his home one did, so she strained to hear anything that would tell her what he was thinking. When he was at work, he always kept a pen in his hand. Tapping it was a sign of impatience; scribbling with it meant he was only half listening. But the pen seemed still.

"Daddy?"

"What about your life here? Your friends?"

She choked back a laugh. "I've learned enough about *true* friendship in the past week to assure me the only real friend I have is Marie, and she's staying."

"Marie is willing to leave New York?" His voice bordered on shrill. "Has she gone crazy?"

"Maybe. I don't know."

"She's not the reason you're wanting to stay, is she? You've always followed her irresponsible impulses. You're not doing it again, are you?"

"No, Dad." Patricia ran her fingers through her hair. "I've prayed about it and . . ."

"You *prayed?*"

"Yes, I prayed. You raised me to be a Christian, remember? Praying is what Christians do when faced with a big decision." She took a breath to settle down. "This is a big decision, and God has granted me a peace about staying here. I think it's the right move."

He sighed. "I can't argue with you *and* God."

The defeat in his voice shattered her resolve. "I can come home if you'd like. I know this is a bad time. You need me–"

"No, no, it's not that. Marcy's doing a fine job. You trained her well."

"But it's going to get crazy–"

"Yes, but it's not bad right now." He paused a moment, probably rubbing the crease in his forehead. "Jake may be right. Maybe it's time for you to spread your wings a bit."

"There's plenty of room to spread my wings out here." She looked beyond the barn to the distant hills. "I know things will get nuts in September. I can come home and help Marcy then."

"September is fine, but I'm betting you'll be home as soon as you discover how hot Texas can be in the summer." A light laugh; a short pause. "I love you."

"I love you too, Daddy." She choked out the words, tears of

homesickness sliding down her cheeks. She swallowed. "Kiss Mom for me."

She sniffed, swiping a finger under her eyes. Before, her longing for home had been just a mild tug; now, it threatened to jerk her heart out through her throat. She swiveled to set the receiver back in its cradle and saw Marie leaning cross-armed against the doorframe.

"And just when were you going to tell me your decision?"

"After I told him." Guilt tugged at Patricia's conscience. She'd never held anything back from Marie.

"How'd he take it?"

"Let's just say he was less than exuberant." She lifted her lips in a slight smile. "He said *you* were crazy."

"He may be right." Marie padded barefoot across the floor to sit in one of the leather chairs facing the desk and draped her long legs over its arm. "Did he manage to talk you out of staying?"

Patricia shook her head. "Not that he didn't try."

"When are you going to tell the men?"

"Before dinner, I guess. I need to catch them before Jack and Randy go home."

"What difference does it make? Just tell the supper crowd. They'll tell the others."

"I need to gauge their reactions." Patricia rolled her chair closer to the dreaded paperwork and folded her arms on the desk. "I think Talon and Chance will be happy, and Frank, but some of the men may not like working for a woman."

"This is the twenty-first century. Men are growing accustomed to female bosses these days."

"Marie, do you see a computer in this room?" She picked up

the phone and wrapped the cord around her hand. "What about this? When was the last time you used one of these?" She gave a light laugh as she replaced the receiver. "Twenty-first century or not, this is a land where the men still say *ma'am* and hold the doors open for women. They may not respond well to having a female boss, especially one who doesn't know what she's doing."

"You have a point." Marie rose and stretched her back. "But you'd better get word to them before the end of the day. Jack and Randy took their trucks out to the back pasture. They'll probably leave by the side gate when they're done."

Patricia chuckled, and Marie paused mid-stretch to stare at her. "What?"

"Do you realize you just used the words *truck, pasture,* and *gate*?"

"What about you? Palpating cows, riding bulls." She grinned. "Didn't take long for us to change, did it?"

"It's a positive change, don't you think? This place will be good for us."

"We'll see how good it is after you've told the men you're staying."

Patricia laughed. "I'll have Chef tell them to come back here after work." She picked up a stack of papers and tamped them on their edges. "What are you doing this afternoon?"

"Shopping for shops. If we're staying, I have to find work. And if I want to get along with *my* boss, I'd better own the store. Want to come?"

Patricia bit her lip and eyed the paperwork. She'd rather go with Marie—she'd rather ride a wild stallion under thorny mesquites—than deal with this business. But if she was going to run the ranch, she'd have to take responsibility. Might as well start now.

Work on the ranch came to a halt at sundown–seven-thirty this time of year. At four-thirty, Patricia had forced down a sandwich and soda, avoiding both Chef and the men. She'd dreaded eating her dinner surrounded by silence and sullen looks if their response to her decision was unfavorable.

She paced the den just outside the dining room door. The men were waiting restlessly while she wrung her hands. How would she break the news? This western world of denim and dirt, cowboy gentlemen and plain-spoken women was entirely alien to her. The social code was different, and she hadn't been here long enough to learn all the nuances.

Should she enter the room with assertiveness, state her decision with an authority she didn't feel? A smile tugged at her lips as she pictured herself, arms akimbo, chin up: *I'm the new boss of this here ranch. Y'all've gotta answer to me now.*

Too bad she didn't chew tobacco. It'd be a great time to spit.

She paced to the windows. Humility would be the better approach. Maybe a touch of humor: *Sorry, guys. You've got a lady boss now. I'm renaming the ranch to Petticoat Farms. No, no, only kidding.*

Ouch.

Ordering herself to get a backbone, she straightened her shoulders, tilted her chin a bit, and strode toward the dining room. She'd approach them with the same respect she'd have for a room full of senators, and the authority of a social coordinator who knew the ropes.

She paused. *Lord, please give me the words.*

Heads turned in her direction as she entered. Chef and Consuela stood at the kitchen door, the men sat on the benches around the table. Marie, bless her, was perched on the uncomfortable straight back chair at the foot of the table, in Patricia's direct line of sight. She slipped Patricia a wink and a smile, giving her a quick nod of encouragement.

"Hi guys, sorry to keep everyone so long." She eyed the men in the room. Randy and Jack didn't meet her gaze. They probably wanted to be home having their dinners. Frank studied her with soft blue eyes surrounded by the crinkles of age; Buster raised his bushy brows in expectation; Chance offered a hesitant grin. Only Talon's eyes were impassive; guarded, perhaps. What was he thinking? She cast a glance to Chef and Consuela; both regarded her with stony faces. "I guess everyone is wondering why I called you in here tonight."

She clamped her sweaty palms behind her back; her shoulder muscles tightened. Closing her eyes, she took a deep breath and whipped out the words. "I've decided to keep the ranch."

A peek to gauge their reaction revealed everyone regarding her much the same as before she'd made her announcement. She stepped closer to Marie, the one soul she knew supported her, and rushed on with her message.

"Nothing is going to change around here, and I'm afraid I won't be much of a boss since I don't know a lot about ranching." A nervous giggle escaped her lips. "Okay, I know *nothing* about ranching. I'm relying on everyone to help me learn. Until I do, Talon is the foreman. You'll be taking orders from him, same as always."

No one responded, but she noticed minute changes in their

faces as the tension eased.

Frank's eyes sparkled as he stroked his whiskers. "You get hooked on that eight-second ride, ma'am?"

She blushed in the ensuing laughter and peeked at Talon through lowered lashes. Relief mingled with the approval in his eyes. His smile warmed her.

He rose from the bench and pulled out the chair at the head of the table. "This is your place, ma'am."

Patricia closed the expense log with a thud and leaned back in the chair. *Finally!* She'd been all the way through each of the ledgers. Thank the good Lord it wasn't information she'd be tested on, because not much of it remained in her head. But at least she'd finished the paperwork and paid a stack of bills. She flicked off the desk light and rubbed her exhausted eyes. She would forego her bath tonight and drop straight into bed.

Someone knocked on the front door, and she groaned. Marie was out with Chance, so Patricia would have to answer it. She heaved herself to her feet and plodded through the house. Talon looked at her through the window in the door. She opened it and offered a tired smile.

"Rough day?"

"To put it mildly." She waved him toward the den and sat down beside him on the battered, striped sofa. "I'm making headway, though."

"Still trying to learn ranching in a day?"

She laughed. "I'm convinced now that's impossible."

"You need a few more hands-on lessons."

He wrapped her hand in his, and she played with his fingers.

"What are your dreams for this place, Talon? You mentioned wanting to go to computers, wanting to raise registered Angus. What else?"

He regarded her for a long time. "I'll tell you my newest dream. I want you to make this place *your* home too. I want to see your signature on it. I want you comfortable here–happy. Not feeling like a guest in your own house." He rose from the sofa, pulling her with him, then turned her to face the den. From behind her, with his hands resting on her shoulders, he lowered his lips to her ear. "Have you looked around here lately?"

She studied the room as if seeing it for the first time. The sofa's yellow-striped fabric was worn thin and stained. Water rings marred one of the side tables; the other listed to the left. The lampshade was dull and brittle. On the blue plaid recliner, the footrest hung off-kilter, and on the chair opposite it, the cushion sagged in the middle.

"It's . . . homey."

"It's *sad.* Did you ever notice the matchbook leveling the table in the dining room?" He turned her toward him. "This place could use a facelift. Most of the furniture in the house has been here since Loretta's dad owned the place. We're talking–what?– forty years? More?" He brushed his hand against her cheek. "The house is yours now. Make it your home."

She twisted around and swept her gaze over the room once more. "I could do that."

"You want to start tomorrow? Work on fixing it up some?"

"Guess we could. Take stock of what we need, what we can afford." She held a finger to her chin. "I could ship in my things from New York. See what would work in here. Maybe Chef and Consuela could use some new dishes and small appliances. It's not like I know how to use them."

"You could learn." He smirked.

A mock-glare was her only response. "What'll we do with the stuff in here?"

"Burn it."

"That would be quite a bonfire." She laughed, but her laughter died and she became serious. "What about the ranch itself? What do you want to do?"

"Can we start by getting a computer?"

"Oh, yes. And cordless phones. And I'd like one more thing."

"What's that?"

She smiled at his puzzled look. "I want to raise Hanoverian Warmblood horses. Maybe open an equestrian school for kids."

"So you *do* have plans of your own. Can the ranch afford it?"

"No. But I can." She rested her hand on his chest. "I want to do this. I don't know much about ranching, but I do know how to train show horses. And teaching something I love would give me a sense of purpose."

"You're going to be a busy lady, then." He tightened his arms around her. "I'd better do this while there's still time."

Her heart fluttered as he lowered his lips to hers. He kissed her with a sweetness that made her want to melt into him, become part of him. She felt a sense of loss when he pulled back, but before she could open her eyes, he kissed her again–deeper, with a longing that matched her own. It felt so right, so perfect, she had the sudden fear she was dreaming. And had no desire to wake up.

But the gravel crunching on the driveway told them Chance

and Marie were home. One more lingering hug, one more sweet kiss, and Talon released her.

Chapter Twenty-Two

Talon lowered Bodine's back left hoof and nudged his horse over in the stable breezeway so he could clean the back right. During the recuperation period for Bodine's injured foreleg, Talon had neglected grooming him, and now his hooves needed a trim. He grabbed the hoof pick and went to work again, humming a tune.

All day, while riding the fence line, he had been singing songs he'd written recently and songs from long past. Any melody that came to his head. He felt lighter than he had in years. Everything he saw seemed clearer, brighter, more colorful. Even after mucking out the stalls, he'd walked with a buoyancy in his step, and a grin just itching to lift his cheeks.

If he closed his eyes, he could still feel the dizzying effects of Pat's lips on his own, still feel her arms sliding around his back and clutching him tighter. But if he closed his eyes, he'd refuse to reopen them. He'd just stay lost in the memory until he could kiss her again.

Maybe God would allow him to fall in love again after all. Maybe this time it would be for keeps.

Chance entered the barn and grabbed his grooming kit from the tack room.

"You've been grinning a lot lately." He slapped Talon's back as he passed toward Molly's stall. "I'd be willing to bet it has something to do with Pat—and I don't mean just her decision to stay."

"It'd be a safe bet." Talon dropped the pick and grabbed the nippers. From behind, he heard a stall door open and the rhythmic thud of hooves on the packed dirt.

"Let me get this straight," Chance said. "Falling in love at first sight is impossible, but give it a couple of weeks and it's okay?"

"Who said anything about love?"

"You're not fooling anyone. It was hard to miss the way you two looked at each other over breakfast this morning."

Talon huffed out a sigh of feigned irritation. "There are no secrets on this ranch."

"Nope." A chuckle accented Chance's response.

For a few moments, the only sounds were Chance's brush sweeping down Molly's back in firm, brisk strokes, and the clack of Talon's nippers on Bodine's hoof—both accompanied by the animals' snorts.

Finally, Chance said, "It's getting late. When do you suppose those women are coming home?"

Talon flipped his wrist over for a look at his watch. "It's only six-thirty. They should be back soon." He grabbed the rasp and grinned at Chance. "You've never been away from your own lady love this long, huh?"

Chance's ears turned red.

Once done with the hoof, Talon released Bodine's leg and

straightened his back with a good stretch. After a final rub on the horse's nose, he led him into his stall, then went to the next one to retrieve Pacer. The four-year-old cutting horse shied from the halter. He was high strung and skittish, so Talon slung an arm around the horse's neck to keep him still. Once the halter was in place, Talon guided him from the stall, closing the gate behind him, and secured the lead rope.

He grabbed a curry comb. Pacer side-stepped away from it, trapping himself between Talon and the stall gate. He stood like a jittery ball of nerves while Talon stroked the rubber nubs along his back. "Did Marie find a place to open her shop?"

"She said she found something promising in town, but since Pat was going to Stephenville, she decided to look there too. What's Pat doing in Stephenville?"

"Furniture shopping, probably. And she has a lot to do to transfer everything here from New York."

"Yeah, Marie does too." Chance dropped the mane comb into his kit and checked Molly's teeth. "After listening to everything she had to do, I'm glad she thinks the effort's worth it. I just hope she doesn't have to go back to New York for any reason."

"Afraid she'll change her mind?"

Chance grinned over Molly's back. "Nah. Afraid she'll ask me to go with her."

Talon had to shove Pacer away from the gate to work on his other side. After brushing him down and working a comb through his mane and tail, all that remained were the hooves. He stooped and leaned against the horse's shoulder until the leg lifted, then settled it between his knees and reached for the hoof pick.

"Chance!" Marie flew into the horse barn, flush-faced and excited. "Chance!"

"Marie–no!" But Pat's warning came too late.

Pacer's ears pricked and his eyes rimmed white. He jerked back on the lead rope and yanked his leg from Talon's grasp, knocking him over. Talon scrambled to get away, but Pacer slammed a hoof against his inner thigh.

"Whoa! Easy, boy." Chance grabbed the rope, positioning himself between the horse and Talon.

With pain shooting through his leg like lightning, Talon scooted away on his backside until he smashed into the front of Bodine's stall. He pulled himself up on the gate slats. Gritting his teeth against a sudden dizziness, he clamped his eyes shut and gave his head a good shake. Soft hands caressed his face. He opened his eyes again to find Pat peering at him.

"You okay?" Her voice quivered.

"Yeah. He got my leg, but I'm okay."

"Let's see."

"Here?" Talon looked around. Pacer was back in his stall. Marie stood with her fist pressed to her lips, encircled by Chance's arm.

"I'm so sorry." Marie's eyes teared. "I just didn't think. I'm so sorry."

"We need to tend to your leg." Pat was in a control-mode unfamiliar to Talon. In spite of the paleness of her face, her voice was commanding, and her movements defied argument. She wrapped his arm around her shoulders, and her arm around his waist. "Let's get you back to the bunkhouse."

Chance stepped forward. "Let me help."

"I have him. Thanks."

Pain radiated through Talon's leg with every step, and his jaw ached from clamping it shut, but with Pat's help, he managed the short walk.

She barreled through the bunkhouse door, leaving it open behind her, and released him in the nearest chair. "Slip your pants down and let's take a look."

He stared at her. "You mean for me to undress? Now? With you here?"

"Oh, good grief, Talon. Just do it." She went to the small refrigerator next to the coffee stand and pulled out the ice bucket from the freezer. Looking around and not finding what she wanted, she disappeared into the bathroom.

The pain in Talon's leg screamed for an ice pack and a couple of Tylenol. He hobbled to his bunk and slid out of his jeans. An angry red imprint marred the inner thigh of his left leg. He would have a good bruise there. Not the first he'd ever had, and probably wouldn't be the last. But it was the first tended to by a woman not considered a mom. He slipped under the covers, propped his back against the wall, and draped the sheets over him, leaving the offended leg exposed.

Pat came to him with the ice bundled in a towel in one hand, and the Tylenol bottle and a glass of water laced in the fingers of the other. She saw his leg and winced. "Hope you didn't pay your entry fees for the rodeo tomorrow night."

"Paid them yesterday." He sucked in his breath when she applied the ice pack. "This shouldn't keep me out of the game."

She gaped at him. "You're not riding like this. You won't be able to stay on the bull!"

"I've ridden with worse. I'll be able to stay on."

"How? Look at this. You've probably bruised the muscle."

"Probably. Which means I'd really like to have the Tylenol now."

She eyed the bottle as if surprised it was there, then handed him the water. Snapping the top off the Tylenol, she asked, "How many?"

"Three."

She shook them into his hand. "You're not going to practice tonight, are you?"

"No."

"Well, at least that's something."

He popped the tablets in his mouth and washed them down with the water, glimpsing the tight set of her lips. She was worried about him. It felt good.

Later in the evening, Patricia greeted Frank and Buster on the opposite side of the dining room table as she slid in beside Chance and Marie. "Where's Talon?"

"Here." Talon's voice came to her from the den. "I'm coming."

She winced at his every move during his slow progression into the dining room. He was dressed in a t-shirt, cut-off jeans, and flip-flops. The ice pack wrapped around his leg with an Ace bandage made even limping awkward for him. He settled on the end of the bench next to Frank and propped his leg on the chair at the foot of the table. His breath whooshed out as if he'd been holding it since he left the bunkhouse.

"Wobblin' like an old man," Frank said.

"Feeling a bit like one."

He had good, strong legs, shocking white under dark hair. Patricia caught herself eyeing his muscular calf. It would only partially help him stay on a bull. He needed his groin muscle.

Give the Lady a Ride

She drew her lips tight and glanced away, ignoring the banter among the men. The very idea that Talon insisted on riding tomorrow night boiled in her stomach like molten metal. Had she not learned how to ride, maybe she wouldn't be so skeptical now. But she *had* learned, and she knew the strain of keeping good balance on the back of a spinning bull. If he thought she'd let the subject drop, he didn't know her very well.

Okay, he *didn't* know her very well–not after just two weeks. Time for his first lesson in Patricia Talbert 101.

"I'm so sorry, Talon." Marie had been beating herself up for her foolish move since it had happened. Patricia knew it would never happen again.

"Don't worry about it, I'll be fine." He treated her to the same genuine smile that had turned Patricia's head the first day they'd met.

Consuela bustled in with a platter of enchiladas and a bowl of refried beans. She put the food on the center of the table and gaped at Talon's outstretched leg. "*¡Dios mío!* What happened?"

"It's nothing, *Mama*. I'll be fine."

"Nothing, he says. Nothing!" She waddled to the den, muttering under her breath, and returned with a worn green throw pillow. The sharp blend of Spanish and English words she spent on Talon while she propped up his leg was nonsensical to Patricia. But the tone wasn't. Whatever Consuela was saying, she agreed wholeheartedly.

When Consuela's hand came to a rest on Talon's shoulder, he took it to his lips to kiss. "Stop fussing."

"If I don't fuss at you, who will?"

Talon shot a glance across the table. "Pat."

Consuela peered at her, the conspiratorial look in her eyes hedged by her drill-sergeant tone. "See that you do."

"It's in the plans." Patricia glared a warning to Talon.

"Leave him alone, he's fine." Chef slid a plate of tortillas and a bowl of rice on the table, glowering at his wife. "Go get the salsa." She frowned at him and left for the kitchen. "You going to ride tomorrow?"

"Of course."

"That's good. You can do it. You're young and tough." He grinned at Patricia. "He's tough. He can do it."

Patricia couldn't bring herself to return his smile. During the supper prayer, she sifted through her mind in search of a convincing argument to talk Talon out of riding. She ate her meal in silence, listening with only half an ear as Marie told everyone she'd found a perfect place to open a shop in Stephenville.

Lord, did You bring me all the way out here to watch him get killed?

Give the Lady a Ride

Chapter Twenty-Three

This arena was new to Patricia and Marie and better than the first one, larger and covered. Fans hummed over clean aluminum benches, and the rails wore a blue paint the shade midnight. But the smells of popcorn and sweet cotton candy, which mingled with the odors of dirt and hide, was the same in both arenas.

Katie waved at them from the third bench, and slid over to give them room. "Come to see your men ride?"

"Wouldn't miss it." Marie sat to Patricia's right and leaned over her to speak to Katie. "Talon's riding hurt."

"What happened?"

"Pacer kicked his leg," Patricia said.

"Ouch. Which one?"

"Left."

"He'll be okay. Especially if he gets a bull that favors his left. A spin to that side will make him rely on his right leg."

Patricia nodded, but her stomach knotted. Talon had brushed away all her arguments last night. By the time he kissed her goodnight, she'd given up and let him think she believed him.

Believed that he'd be all right during the next three nights, when he would face bulls larger and meaner than anything the Circle Bar owned.

Talon climbed into the chute and settled down on a red Hereford mix. Pat had worn a furrow in her brow all day, and though she hadn't mentioned it again, she'd made her worry known. After this weekend, he wouldn't put her through this again. He'd settle into ranching and leave the bulls for younger men.

Chance straddled the spinning bull in the arena, but Talon anchored his gaze on his fist in the bull rope. He needed to concentrate on business. The crowd's moan just a split-second before the buzzer told him all he needed to know about Chance's ride.

"Seven point eight seconds," the announcer said. "That hurts, but that's the game. Give the cowboy a round of applause, ladies and gentlemen."

With his hand secure in the rope, Talon worked forward to the bull's shoulders.

"Next up, in chute two, is Talon Carlson on Burnt Biscuit," the deep voice reverberated though the speakers. "He's a tough bull raised by our own Ben Kilgore of the Flying K. This is the first time we've seen Biscuit, but Ben promises us a good show."

"You ready?" Buster clapped his shoulder.

"Ya betcha!"

Talon ground his teeth into the mouth guard and nodded to the gateman.

Burnt Biscuit erupted from the chute like spewing lava. Talon rode high on his back, his free hand whipping the air. The bull plowed the ground when his front hooves landed. A fierce twist of the animal's hindquarters pitched Talon off balance. He squeezed with his legs and hung on. As soon as the back hooves hit the dirt, the bull launched again, all fours flying over the sand. Coiling back on the landing, Biscuit started his spin to the left with a savage toss of his flank. Pain shot through Talon's injured leg as he listed. His wrist twisted at an awkward angle. Fire burned through his muscles as he strained to hold on.

His balance was off, and the bull seemed to know it. Biscuit made one final back-wrenching leap. The buzzer pierced the air just as Talon flew off. Biscuit was too close to the chutes. Talon was flying toward a gate. He threw his arms out to catch a slat, but his right arm missed and shot between the rails. Inside the chute, a bull reared and slammed against the gate.

Mind-searing pain exploded in Talon's arm.

Patricia watched from the stands with her fists pressed to her lips. Talon sprawled at the base of chute three, his body twisted like scrap metal. He didn't move.

In an instant, cowboys surrounded him, guarded him, watched Biscuit's every move. At the center of the arena floor, the bull lowered his blunt horns and charged a bullfighter. Watching the animal from over his shoulder, a wrangler ran in front of him and lead him away from Talon and toward the back alley, then jumped the rails as he neared the gate. Two more bullfighters flanked Biscuit from behind and chased him through the opening, and the gateman slammed off any idea of retreat the bull may have had.

The emergency team entered the arena, blocking Patricia's

view of Talon. When she could see him again, he was strapped to a stretcher carried by four men.

"Let's go." Katie's voice sounded distant. "Pattie! Let's go!"

Patricia walked in a daze between Katie and Marie. She felt numb, but somehow her legs kept moving. Her purse hung over her shoulder, but she didn't remember grabbing it. Had Marie put it there? She dug out her keys, but her hands shook so hard she dropped them.

"I'll drive." Marie picked up the keys, then wrapped an arm around Patricia's shoulders. "Katie, do you want to ride with us?"

Patricia didn't catch the response, hearing instead the wail of a siren.

Chapter Twenty-Four

In the emergency room waiting area, Patricia's boots clunked across the highly polished floor. Funny how they didn't *click* like her high heels did. Would she ever need high heels again?

What was taking them so long?

From the swinging door that separated her from Talon, she paced back to Marie and Katie. "Do you think they'd tell us if he needed surgery?"

"We're not family." Marie shifted on the yellow plastic seat. "With the privacy policies these days, they may not be able to."

Katie lowered the tattered copy of *Western Horseman* to her lap. "Try not to worry, Pat. They'll let us see him soon."

The glass entrance into the ER swooshed open, and Chance, Buster, and Frank filed in.

Frank went straight for Patricia and wrapped her in his arms. "You okay, kiddo?"

His wiry frame felt like a granite pillar. She wanted to cling to him, draw on his strength, but she released him after a quick hug to keep from crying again. "I think so. But we don't know anything yet." She looked at Buster. "You were at his chute, weren't you? What happened?"

Buster took his hat off and rubbed a hand over his bald spot. "Biscuit threw him against the chute. He hit his head, busted his arm. He was unconscious when they carried him out."

Patricia tightened her lips against a whimper. Why wouldn't they let her see him?

"He's going to be all right, Pat," Chance said. "He's tough. He'll be fine."

She whirled toward him. "That's what you said before he climbed on that bull. *He's tough. He'll be fine.* But he's not fine!"

Frank reached for her again, but she twisted away. "It's insane! Riding a bull when you're healthy is hard enough, but to ride injured? It's ludicrous! And all of you supported him. Encouraged him. And now he's . . ." Her voice cracked. She swiped angry tears from her eyes and turned her back on the lot of them.

"Patricia Talbert?"

A young male nurse in green scrubs scanned the group in the waiting room. Straightening her back to steel herself against another wave of fear, Patricia said, "I'm Patricia Talbert."

The nurse's rubber-soled shoes squeaked on the linoleum as he moved closer to her. "We're going to move Talon to a room for tonight–just for observation–but he wanted to see you now."

He led the way through the double doors. Without a backward glance, she followed.

Once in the inner sanctum of the ER, she asked, "Is he going to be all right?"

"He has a mild concussion and a broken arm, but he'll be just fine." He turned right, leading her down a corridor flanked by canvas cubicles on one side and a bustling nurses' station on the other. "He may be a bit loopy when you see him—if he's awake at all. He's on Vicodin."

She stepped aside for another nurse wheeling a crash cart at a quick clip down the hall. "Vicodin is for pain?"

"Yes, ma'am." He pulled aside a curtain, second from the end of the hall, peeked inside, and smiled. "I think he's out of it."

"If it's okay, I'd like to stay with him."

The nurse held the curtain open for her, then disappeared when she went inside.

She walked softly to Talon's bedside. "Talon?"

He lay on the white sheet with his arm, now in a cast from his wrist to his elbow, resting on his stomach. An IV dripped saline into the tube leading to his good arm.

His hair was mussed, his eyes closed, and his lips parted with drug-induced sleep. He looked like a little boy, napping after his playtime. She caressed his wavy hair and felt the lump on his head that promised to hurt him for days to come.

A straight-back chair rested against the curtained divider between Talon's cubical and the adjacent one. She dragged it to his bedside and sat. Resting her hand on his good arm, she watched his face while he slept.

The sun rose, casting a dull light against the air conditioner unit outside Talon's third-floor window. Patricia watched it brighten the horizon for a few moments longer, then dropped the curtain and turned back to the darkened room.

Talon had slept through everyone's visit. Katie and Marie had ridden home with Chance, leaving Patricia's rented Mercedes in the parking lot. She couldn't even remember where they parked last night.

Smoothing the sheet over Talon's chest, she looked down at his sleeping face. He'd had a fitful night, waking occasionally in pain, once while the nurse was in the room. She left for a moment, then returned with a syringe and emptied its contents into a port on the IV tube. A little something for the pain, she'd said.

Patricia spent the night in a chair not much more comfortable than the plastic ones in the ER. She hadn't prayed during the night, still too angry. He was going to be fine, the doctor had said. He'd probably go home today. At the doctor's words, a wave of relief had washed over her.

But as the night wore on, the anger grew. Talon was so *stubborn*. And he seemed to have very little regard for her feelings. She'd done all she could before the ride to plead and argue him out of it. When that didn't work, she had prayed. But God took his side. Or Talon had ignored Him. Either way, frustration ate at her stomach for most of the night, while Talon slept off his pain in oblivion. Every time he moaned, she found herself torn between sympathy and irritation. *Serves you right*, she'd think, then rise to stroke his forehead.

Sometime during the early hours of the morning, her anger melted. Talon was a man of faith. He prayed before he rode, and trusted God to pull him through. Maybe that was what gave him the courage to ride injured.

She wanted to be able to trust God like that. To cut a hole in the safety net, as Marie once said, and fall through. The decision to move to Texas was a big one, but as long as there were planes to take her back to New York, it was still a *safe* decision. She needed to do something big, the outcome of which was beyond her control and in God's hands.

Two weeks ago, Talon had asked what gave her the greatest sense of accomplishment. She didn't have an answer then, but now she did. Everything she'd done at the ranch was an accomplishment. She'd met every challenge head-on and succeeded.

Except riding Mostro.

Her adrenaline spiked at the very thought of the steer. Her desire to ride him probably equaled Talon's desire to ride one of the Flying K bulls. She wanted to pray before her ride and trust God to keep her safe. But she wanted more than that. She wanted to trust Him, to give herself completely to Him, and tell Him, *Do with me as You will.*

An idea formed in her mind, and she straightened with the resolve to see it through.

Give the Lady a Ride

Chapter Twenty-Five

Saturday afternoon, with the Vicodin wearing off and the pain snaking back into his consciousness, Talon rode home in the passenger seat of the Mercedes. He wasn't used to being chauffeured by a woman, but as he shifted his head on the neckrest to look at her, he had to admit he couldn't complain about the view. Even tired, she was beautiful.

Pat's silent times weren't triggered just by Talon's truck. She was quiet in the car too. Must be the thrum of the tires on the pavement that lulled her into a hush.

But she wasn't just tired; something weighed heavy on her mind. She gave her lips a hard time–drawing them tighter than a fence line one second, attacking them with her teeth the next. Was she mad he'd ridden in spite of her protests? He couldn't blame her. Watching him get injured couldn't have been easy for her. She was probably furious he hadn't listened to her. He should have. He should've given her fears the respect they deserved. Riding injured was nothing new for him, so he hadn't been concerned. But he should've realized she didn't share that confidence.

Should he say something? Apologize?

In just two weeks, he'd learned to admire her grit, her determination. He'd drifted from attraction to infatuation. He'd seen her happy, worried, thoughtful, jealous. Even mad a time or two. There were times he felt he knew her.

This was not one of those times.

He didn't know whether to open his mouth or just ride out her mood. But watching her grip the wheel with one hand and twirl tangles into her hair with the other made him lean toward apologizing.

"Pat . . ."

"I want to ride Mostro."

He blinked. The whole time he was beating himself up, she'd been thinking about *riding*? Her tone was neutral; he couldn't tell what she had in mind. "Why?"

Her eyes darted to him, then back to the road. Her brows pinched over her nose, but not in anger. It was . . . He didn't know what it was.

A year slipped by before she spoke. "Do you pray before you ride?"

"Of course."

"Do you ask for success or safety?"

"Both."

"And you trust God to answer, right?"

"Yeah, I do." Where was this going?

She turned down the ranch road and pulled over in the grass. After putting the car in park and shutting off the engine, she shifted to face him.

"I want to trust Him like that. I want to test myself and see if

Give the Lady a Ride

I can do it. The ride, I mean." She glanced out the windshield. "No, that's not true. It's both. I want to see if I can ride Mostro, *and* I want to test my faith. I want to pray before the ride and accept whatever happens." She looked at him again, her eyes serious. "Do you understand?"

He huffed out a breath. "Yeah, I think so. I'll tell the men. We can get you on that steer tomorrow."

"No. I want to ride today, before I lose my nerve."

"Can't let you do that. You've been up all night."

She crossed her arms. "So, the man who rode injured is telling me I can't ride tired? I'm not hurt anywhere, Talon, I have no injuries. I think I can do it."

"You've ridden Mostro twice after a long day of work. He dropped you in the dust both times."

"But it won't be much of a test if I'm well rested."

"Oh, yes it will. Mostro isn't like Bart. He's not used to being ridden. Not used to humans. He's wild. You'll have to be able to give a hundred percent to make the eight, and you can't do that handicapped with fatigue."

She lowered her eyes and picked at a speck on her jeans before returning her gaze to his. "I want the flank strap on him."

"The ride will be dangerous enough without it."

"I'm not negotiating. If I have to wait until tomorrow, I want the flank strap."

"I can't talk you out of it?"

"No." She took his hand, lacing her fingers with his. "Your faith is stronger than mine. You trust God, don't you? Trust Him in this."

Staring at her fingers wrapped around his own, Talon felt his heart wrench in his chest. He trusted God for his own safety. But

233

he'd lost so many loves in his life . . . could he trust Him for hers?

Conversation stopped short at the breakfast table when Patricia entered the room Sunday morning. Everyone smiled at her, but their stares harbored questions. Talon's eyes, usually bright and full of life, looked dull with fatigue.

"Hear you're going to ride today." Buster pushed a bowl of scrambled eggs closer to her place at the head of the table.

"You know what they say. A girl's gotta do what a girl's gotta do." She sat and bypassed the eggs in favor of toast. Her stomach felt as jumpy as an active popcorn popper. Nerves. "How is your arm, Talon?"

"I reckon as long as it's still attached, it's fine." He waited until the chuckles died down. "Chance took first last night."

Chance's ears reddened. "I rank third overall for this weekend."

"You'll take over first tonight and win the purse." Marie beamed at him. "You're the best rider out there. Friday's loss was just a fluke."

With her eyes on her plate, Patricia munched on the slice of dry toast and followed it with a sip of the coffee. She'd slept only five hours last night. The rest of the time she spent in prayer.

Chance said something she missed, and everyone laughed. She looked up to find Frank staring at her. He jerked his head toward the door, then rose from the table and headed for the den. She grabbed her coffee mug and followed.

"Walk with me." Frank lifted his straw hat from the stand and opened the front door for her.

"Where are we going?"

"Not far. Just to the holding pen." As they walked, he settled his hat on his head, reached to his shirt pocket, then hooked his thumbs in his belt loops. "Talon said you have a particular reason for wanting to ride Mostro."

"He did?" Some of her coffee sloshed out of her cup and onto her hand. She transferred the cup to the other hand and slung the tepid drops off.

"He didn't mean to break your trust or anything." Frank looked at her from beneath his hat brim. "You gotta understand, ma'am. There ain't many secrets in a bunkhouse. Come three o'clock in the morning, even the most tight-lipped man is likely to talk a little."

"I guess I worried him."

"A bit, judging from the restless night he had."

"So, he told you why I want to ride?"

"In a way." Frank opened the pasture gate and closed it behind them, then walked her toward the chute pen. "He says you're having a faith crisis. Is that so?"

She lowered her head and nodded.

They went through another gate and crossed the packed dirt of the chute pen that doubled as their riding arena. A pipe rail fence separated the chute pen from the holding pen, where the practice bulls and steers chewed their cud. They watched Patricia and Frank with disinterested eyes. Just to her right, on the other side of the fence, the ground had been stomped and churned into muck around a decimated hay bale. The men would have to release the animals or toss in another bale soon.

Patricia waved off a fly and wrinkled her nose at the stench created by the five head of cattle in the holding pen. Mostro was one of the five. He swiveled his head toward her and blinked before looking away again. How serene he seemed now. How docile. But she wasn't fooled.

Frank propped a boot on the lower rail and crossed his arms over the top one. "Hard to believe how fierce they can be, ain't it?"

"All except Bart."

He snorted. "Well, he has his moments."

She took a sip of her coffee and waited, somewhat surprised with herself. Frank brought her out here for a reason, but he took his time telling her what it was. In New York, she would've crossed her arms over her chest and tapped her foot, demanding he come to the point. But here, she was content to let him do this his way. Another change in her personality she could appreciate.

"My Margie was a great woman. Tough and tender at the same time. Loved this ranch. We had a place of our own in town then, but she came out every chance she got. Put her hands to mending when it was needed, or helping with the birthing when that was needed. We went together like boots and spurs." He shot her a half-grin. "I was the boots."

"Sounds like I would have liked her."

"You would've." His eyes clouded, and he glanced away toward the distant hill beyond the horse pasture and hay barn. "God took her when she was just fifty-five. No warning. She just turned to say something to me one day and dropped dead where she stood. Aneurysm ruptured in her brain."

Patricia's heart lodged in her throat. She rested a hand on his arm. "I'm so sorry."

Give the Lady a Ride

"Yeah, well, so am I. We were married thirty-four years." Frank lowered his head for a moment, then turned to face her. Remnants of pain lingered in his expression. "I couldn't get used to her being gone. I think I came to work with a hangover every day for a couple of years after that. Hated God. Had no use for Him. Jake and Loretta nursed me through all that, brought me back around to my faith."

He pushed off from the rail. "Guess what I'm saying is, I know what a crisis in faith is like. I know what you're going through."

"Then you understand why I have to ride?"

"I'm not sure. That's why I wanted to talk to you." He shoved his hands into his hip pockets. "If you're wanting to ride to prove something to yourself, you don't have to. You just need to look at how much you accomplished in the few weeks you've been here. You did things most city folks would turn tail and run from. And you did 'em good."

Hearing that from him meant a lot. "Thank you."

"Well, you did. And I'm proud of you." He turned serious. "But I tell you this, if you're wanting to ride to test God's love for you, you're making a mistake. He loves you. That's a fact you can count on. Don't go insulting Him by wanting Him to prove it."

It was her turn to study the distant hill. Had she accepted that God loved her? Having Him prove it hadn't crossed her mind. Such a fine line between Frank's words and what was in her heart.

But in the end, she shook her head. "No, it's not that. I'm not testing Him. I'm testing myself. I want the kind of faith Talon has. That Jake and Loretta had. I don't know any other way to get it."

He chuckled. "That's a little like swimming lessons."

"Swimming lessons?"

"Sure. You can go to your lessons two or three times a week like the kids do today and learn the slow way. Or you can learn like I did. Get thrown in the deep end with orders to sink or swim. Ain't pretty, but it works."

"So, you think I'm throwing myself into the deep end?"

"Yes, ma'am. Sounds like it." He wrapped an arm around her shoulders and walked her back toward the house. "Let's get you ready to ride."

"Frank?"

"Hmm?"

"Don't call me ma'am."

Give the Lady a Ride

Chapter Twenty-Six

Pat marched into the arena with a look Talon had seen on her face before. All business.

She flashed a smile at everyone. "I'm ready."

"No, you're not." Talon said.

"Well, I don't have my glove and vest, but–"

"That's not what I'm talking about." Talon slid his good arm around her and drew her closer to Marie and the ranch hands.

The crowd circled around her.

"I wish you'd just learn to cook," Consuela huffed. "You cause me much worry."

"Hush, woman." Chef scowled at his wife, then grinned at Pat. "She's young, she's strong. She can do this."

Pat eyed him. "Sounds like the same words you used before Talon's ride."

"And he's still standing," Buster said. "You'll be fine."

"Of course you will." Marie reached for her hand.

The men removed their hats as everyone drew nearer to Pat. Each one placed a hand on her back and shoulders.

Talon bowed his head. "Lord, we ask your blessings on us this day, and especially on Pat as she rides. You know what's in her heart. You know how she longs to have complete faith in You. Help her make the eight, Lord, and bring her out safely on the other side, strengthened by Your love. It's in Your holy name we pray. Amen."

"Thank you," Pat croaked, blinking misty eyes.

Talon kissed her hair and gave her a quick one-armed hug, then stepped back so the others could do the same. His heart tightened like a fist in a bull rope. *Please keep her safe, Lord.*

Frank pulled the glove out of his pocket and handed it to her, then held the vest open for her to slip into.

"Okay, you're ready." Smiling with what he hoped was confidence, Talon took her elbow and led her around to the platform. Frank followed.

As Chef, Consuela, and Marie cleared out of the arena, Chance and Buster prodded Mostro into the chute. The steer rammed blunted horns into the head gate and sent his hind hooves flying. Pat jerked back from the rail.

"He'll settle in a minute." Frank pulled the tape from his shirt pocket. "Get your glove on."

Watching Frank tape the glove onto Pat's wrist, Talon bit back a wave of fear. This was as much a test for him as it was for her. He wanted to believe God had chosen her for him, but he'd believed the same about Janet. He couldn't live through another loss like that.

Pat stretched and loosened up while Frank helped with the ropes. After the flank strap was on and the bull rope wrapped loosely behind Mostro's shoulders, Chance climbed onto the chute gate. He held the end of the bull rope and grinned at Pat. "Ready?"

Give the Lady a Ride

The fist on Talon's heart squeezed tighter. He wanted to whisk her away from the chute, shove her into the Mercedes, and send her back to New York. Better to have her alive and gone than dead in the arena.

He choked back his fears.

"Keep your mind in the game, lady. Feel it. Head up, chin down. Heels in, toes out. Keep your free hand up and don't let it touch the bull. Get the rhythm." His voice cracked. "Get 'er done."

She nodded, tilted her head to kiss him, and whispered, "Don't worry. I can do this."

Taking a deep breath, she turned to climb into the chute.

Don't worry, she'd said.

Looking down at her nemesis, Patricia vented her breath in a controlled stream. She *could* do this. Her adrenaline obliterated the fatigue left over from yesterday. Talon's prayer fortified her. The love everyone had shown warmed her. She could do this.

She straddled the rail and rested a boot on Mostro's back. He snorted. Adding a bit more pressure, she tensed, keeping a tight grip on the rail and her eyes on the broad head beneath her. The steer pawed the ground.

Patricia waited. When Mostro stilled, she reached across for the gate rail, then brought her leg over. She hovered over the steer, stretched across the chute like a human X, with her gaze glued to his body.

Frank stretched over from behind the chute and grasped her vest. "Ready when you are."

Patricia nodded. Mostro seemed calmer, so she lowered herself onto his back. He shifted his weight. Patricia stiffened, relaxing only when she felt him settle. Whipping her hand down the bull rope, she worked the rosin into her leather glove, then rested it palm up on the strap behind Mostro's shoulder.

The steer was unpredictable. He had exploded from the chute differently each time she rode him. But that was a good thing. If she didn't know what to expect, she couldn't anticipate. She would have to feel it, just as Talon had said. There was no other choice.

The steer bellowed as she squirmed up his back to his broad shoulders. It was a blessing he didn't buck her in the chute, but she hoped he'd put on a good show once Chance pulled the gate. Another ride like the one on Black Bart and she'd never be able to show her face again.

She pounded her fist in the rope once more and gave the nod.

Mostro lurched from the chute, jerking her backward and jarring her spine. Patricia gritted her teeth against the pain and yanked on the bull rope to stay upright. A twisting leap. Patricia tilted, tightened her leg muscles to stay aboard.

Dust clouds rose when the steer's hooves pounded the dry arena. He swerved and kicked at a fence post. Patricia swayed, but balanced an instant before he tossed his hindquarters. The bucking broke into a furious leftward spin. She listed; her riding arm strained to make the adjustment. The animal stumbled, flinging her forward. With only her riding hand, Patricia pushed herself upright against his bulky shoulders.

Mostro gained his footing and charged the fence between the arena and the holding pen. His sudden stop, his violent kick, sent Patricia flying over the rails.

Give the Lady a Ride

Talon's heart slammed against his chest. The practice bulls were still in the holding pen. He gripped the rail with his good hand as Mostro flung Pat into the other pen. The animals fled from the fence rails. Pat landed with an ugly belly flop and lay supine in the muck.

The world stopped. Talon could see nothing but Pat's body lying motionless in the adjacent pen.

"Get her outta there!" Buster shouted, and activity returned to Earth.

Talon stood paralyzed while the men raced to Pat. He couldn't get himself to move, couldn't wrap his brain around what was happening. All his mind could grasp was that Pat was down.

Buster and Chance jumped the fence and scrambled to Pat's side. They rolled her body face-up and lifted her over to Frank, then climbed back again as Frank lowered her to the ground.

She didn't move.

"*¡Dios mío!*"

Chef shoved through the arena gate and raced to Mostro just as the animal turned to charge the small circle of men around Pat. Yelling *Toro! Toro!* like a diminutive matador and waving his short arms, the Mexican distracted the bull and drew him to the opposite corner of the arena from where Pat lay. Buster and Chance sprinted over and soon the three of them herded the steer out.

Talon's eyes shot back to Pat. She sat up and leaned into Frank, lifting her hand to her head.

With a one-armed vault over the rails, Talon dropped into the arena. Ignoring the pain in his leg from Pacer's kick, he flew to her side. Covered hair-to-boot in muck and mud, she was still the most beautiful thing he'd ever seen.

And she was okay. She'd be okay. Wind knocked out of her, probably. But she'd be okay.

"Did I make the time?" she asked.

"Yes ma'am, I believe you did." Frank pulled the stopwatch from his shirt pocket to show her and beamed like a proud papa. "Eight point two seconds."

Talon dropped to his knees beside her.

Her teeth gleamed white against her muddy face. "I did it!"

Finding the cleanest place on her head, Talon kissed her hair. "Yes, ma'am, you sure did."

Patricia had drained the water heater to get the smell of dirt and manure out of her hair.

She'd done it. She had made the eight. On Mostro!

But that success paled in comparison to the awe building in her chest. God loved her. She hadn't meant for her ride to be a test of His love, but now she realized she couldn't test her faith in Him without testing His love for her.

Frank's words popped into her mind. Had she insulted God?

"I'm sorry, Lord," she whispered. "I'm so sorry. But I'm also grateful You love me enough to endure my foolishness."

Her heart was light as she stood in front of her closet, wrapped in a towel. She'd be glad when her clothes arrived from New York. She was running out of things to wear.

A glance at the clock told her she had fifteen minutes before church services. She needed every second of it.

She grabbed a turquoise Oxford shirt and a clean pair of jeans, dressed quickly, then slipped her bare feet into her loafers.

Give the Lady a Ride

Loretta's Bible waited for her on the night stand, and she caressed it before tucking it under her arm. Would Aunt Loretta be proud of her?

Her growling stomach reminded her she hadn't finished her toast earlier. It was a wonder the hunger pains hadn't rumbled loud enough to be heard outside. She snatched her purse off a chair and headed down for a bite.

In the kitchen, she found a pink gift bag sitting on the Formica-topped table. A folded page peeked from the top of the bag, and she lifted it out. It was from Talon.

Her heart felt buoyant as she opened the note and read.

> Been a long time since I felt like this—
> Figured God didn't want me to.
> But my Heavenly Father knew what I missed
> And I had some waiting to do.
>
> Then the day arrived when you came up my drive.
> I took one look and I reckoned
> This ain't the one He meant for me—
> Just not the type I would beckon.
>
> What a woman you turned out to be.
> Nothing like what I suspected.
> With daring and grit, you proved to me
> You're the cowgirl I never expected.
>
> "This is the one," said a voice from above,
> And I can't argue with that.
> He's finally given me someone to love—
> Patricia, my lady, my Pat.

"Aren't you going to look in the bag?"

Behind her, Talon leaned against the doorframe, his arm in a sling and that lopsided grin she loved on his face.

"Thank you for this." She cleared her husky voice, forcing out the emotions lodged in her throat. "You wrote this?"

"That one and several others. It's cowboy poetry. Not Shakespeare, but it's the best I can do."

"It's better than Shakespeare."

He pointed at her mid-section. "We're fixin' to baptize your best friend, and you're not even dressed yet."

Puzzled, she glanced down. Shirt, jeans, shoes.

He stepped closer. "Open the bag."

Cradled in tissue paper was a tooled leather belt with turquoise inlays. She fingered the simple silver buckle. "But I thought Wilson said it would be a month."

"I'd asked him to rush it, and he got it to me before the rodeo last Friday night. Consider it your prize." He cupped her chin. "I'm proud of you."

His smokey-eyed look warmed the pit of her stomach. He slid his hand around her neck, and took possession of her lips with a kiss full of love, promise, desire.

Neon green flashed behind her closed lids.

Patricia Talbert, this is the man I have chosen for you.

CPSIA information can be obtained at www.ICGtesting.com
Printed in the USA
LVOW060740260212

270433LV00001B/66/P